A Bargained-For Bride

Also by Marcia Lynn McClure and available from Center Point Large Print:

Dusty Britches
Weathered Too Young
The Windswept Flame
The Visions of Ransom Lake
The Heavenly Surrender
The Light of the Lovers' Moon
Beneath the Honeysuckle Vine
The Whispered Kiss
The Stone-Cold Heart of Valentine Briscoe
The Highwayman of Tanglewood
A Cowboy for Christmas

A Bargained-For Bride

MARCIA LYNN McCLURE

Center Point Large Print
Thorndike, Maine

This Center Point Large Print edition
is published in the year 2019 by arrangement with
Distractions Ink.

All character names and personalities in this work of fiction are entirely fictional, created solely in the imagination of the author. Any resemblance to any person living or dead is coincidental.

The text of this Large Print edition is unabridged.
In other aspects, this book may vary
from the original edition.
Printed in the United States of America
on permanent paper.
Set in 16-point Times New Roman type.

ISBN: 978-1-64358-231-3

Library of Congress Cataloging-in-Publication Data

Names: McClure, Marcia Lynn, author.
Title: A bargained-for bride / Marcia Lynn McClure.
Description: Large Print edition. | Thorndike, Maine : Center Point Large Print, 2019.
Identifiers: LCCN 2019013348 | ISBN 9781643582313 (hardcover : alk. paper)
Subjects: LCSH: Large type books. | GSAFD: Love stories.
Classification: LCC PS3613.C36 B37 2019 | DDC 813/.6—dc23
LC record available at https://lccn.loc.gov/2019013348

To Jillian,
Ten years ago, something caught your eye
at the county fair—
just a simple book with horses on the cover.
Ten years ago, someone caught my eye
at the county fair—
a kind young girl who touched my heart
and lingered there forever.
Happy Friendship 10th Anniversary
to you and me!

To my hero and inspiration . . .
Kevin from Heaven!

CHAPTER ONE

Jilly smiled as Jack placed a small bouquet of freshly picked wildflowers in her hands as he kissed her cheek.

"And don't you look pretty today, Jilly Adams?" he flirted.

"Why, thank you, Jack Taylor," Jilly answered. She blushed cherry-red with delight. Jack Taylor was not only the most handsome young man in town but also by far the most charming. "You're lookin' very handsome yourself today," she added. After all, a flattering compliment the likes Jack always offered must be reciprocated.

Jack smiled, obviously pleased by Jilly's favorable remark—and it was an honest observation. Jack Taylor was tall, with broad shoulders, splendidly blue eyes, thick black hair, and a smile that melted the knees of every girl in town—including Jilly's. In truth, Jilly felt not only overjoyed but also very honored that Jack had fallen in love with her. After all, there were other young ladies in the small town of Mourning Dove that were pretty—young ladies prettier than Jilly. The Havasham sisters, for instance—the three daughters of Doctor and Mrs. Havasham—now they were beautiful! Mona, Dina, and Inola were all three raven-haired beauties with dark brown eyes and skin like flawless porcelain, and all three were of eligible age for courting and marriage. Yet the good-looking Jack Taylor had chosen to give his heart to Jilly Adams—so why shouldn't she be proud?

"Wanna join me for an amble?" Jack asked.

"Of course," Jilly answered, her smile broadening.

"I thought we'd head down to the crick today," he explained. "Ya know? Just dangle our feet in the water and cool off for a bit."

"How very refreshin'," Jilly giggled as they began to walk toward the creek.

"There might even be some tadpoles still lingerin' in the standin' water near the bank," he added with a wink.

"If we're lucky," Jilly said. "Summer is movin' on far too quickly for my likin'. But tadpoles always mean there's still some time left for enjoyin' the sunshine and warm weather."

Jack winked at Jilly as he lowered his voice and said, "And I do plan to enjoy this warm weather with you, Jilly Adams . . . as thoroughly as I can."

Jilly shook her head, blushed, and giggled with delight. Jack was so wonderful! She couldn't wait to get down to the creek and find a private spot so that Jack could steal a kiss from her. It was his way, what he always did when they were alone—stole several kisses from Jilly until her confidence grew enough so that he didn't have to steal them anymore.

Yet sometimes Jilly wondered if she really should spend so much time sparking with Jack. She knew that most girls in town had never been kissed at all—yet Jilly had become quite familiar with Jack's kisses. But as the mere thought of Jack kissing her caused her heart to leap in her bosom, Jilly shrugged away her worries. And besides, even her own grandmother had been telling Jilly tales of the way she and Jilly's grandfather used to spark when they first started courting. Thus, Jilly figured that if her Grandma Effie and Grandpa Doolin did a measure of sparking before they were married, then what was wrong with sparking a bit with Jack Taylor?

"I love summer," Jack remarked as they walked down the grassy hill of Mr. Ramsey's west pasture. "I can't hardly make myself look forward to harvesttime and then winter."

"Oh, but harvesttime isn't so bad," Jilly offered. "Everything is mellowed somehow. The sun shines rather orange instead of yellow, the crops come in, everyone starts burnin' cedar and apple wood in their fireplaces." Jilly smiled as a feeling of happiness in anticipation began to well up inside her. "Oh, I just love the scents in the evenin' air in the autumn of the year."

But Jack laughed. "That's because you ain't the one who has to chop all the wood for the fireplaces or haul in all the corn and pumpkins, tomatoes, and such. All you have to do is sit there in your granny's parlor and do nothin'."

"That is not true, Jack Taylor!" Jilly playfully scolded. "And you know it. Who do you think puts up all the jars of jams and jellies, stewed tomatoes, corn, and green beans? Not you men, that's for sure."

Jack nodded as he laughed. "I'll give you that," he agreed. "And where you like the smell of the firewood, I like the smell in my mama's kitchen when she's preservin'."

"My, yes!" Jilly confirmed. She stopped walking a moment, closed her eyes, and said, "If I stand real still, I can almost see the blackberries simmerin' on my grandma's stove. I can almost hear that sound when she pours in the sugar and begins stirrin' with her biggest and best wooden spoon. Oh, I can't wait to smell the blackberries simmerin' this year!"

"Now, don't be wishin' my summer away, Silly Jilly," Jack said, taking her hand. Jilly opened her eyes once more to see Jack smiling at her. "Now come on. We don't have too much time before I gotta be home to milk the cows."

Jilly nodded with understanding, clinging to Jack's hand as they hurried down the hill. She couldn't help but think of the old nursery rhyme her mother had taught her as a child—the one about Jack and Jill going up a hill—only she was glad that she and Jack weren't tumbling down toward the creek.

As ever, a twinge of sadness and heartache pricked Jilly's heart at the thought of her mother. She wondered—as she always did whenever she lingered in thinking of her mother and father—what her life would be like if her parents hadn't been killed, if the bridge over the gorge hadn't collapsed, sending their train plummeting more than a thousand feet into the Arkansas River below. She wondered if she would've been happier with her parents—even happier than she'd been being raised by her Grandma Effie and Grandpa Doolin. She wondered if she would've had siblings, a little brother or sister, or both.

But as she always did when heartache and doubt began to seep into her thoughts, Jilly sighed, inhaled a deep breath, forced a smile to her pretty face, and returned to being conscious of the moment she was living in then—abandoning the wondering of how that moment might have been different had her parents not been killed when she was four years old.

Jack's whistle of astonishment drew Jilly from her deeper thoughts.

"Look at that!" he exclaimed, gesturing to the creek. "It must be rainin' pretty hard somewhere up in the mountains. I've never seen this crick so swollen."

Jilly nodded as a small wave of trepidation traveled through her at the sight of the unusually high quantity of water racing down the creek. "I guess we won't be finding any tadpoles lingerin' about," she said, trying to ease her anxiety.

The creek was far more full than Jilly had ever seen it before—at least three feet above the normal water line. She could see the soft green grass, usually just at the edge of the water, bent over and drowning two or three feet beneath the surface now. Jilly wasn't sure why—though she suspected it had something to do with the train accident that had plunged her parents into the Arkansas River, killing them—but deep or fast-moving water entirely unsettled her.

Yet as she began nervously fiddling with the brooch at the front of her shirtwaist collar, she felt Jack take her hand once more.

He was smiling with understanding when she looked up to him. "Don't worry, Jilly," he encouraged. "We'll stay clear of the water today, okay? We won't even go near the pond."

"Okay," Jilly sighed with relief.

"In fact," Jack mumbled, glancing around to ensure their privacy, "I think a little kissin' might be just what ol' Doc Havasham might recommend in a situation like this. Hmmm?"

Jilly giggled with delight as Jack then led her to

a more secluded part of the creek bank—a small grove of dogwood trees flourishing nearby.

"Now," he began, putting his hands at Jilly's waist and pulling her close, "I'm pretty sure I can settle down your worryin' a bit here."

Jilly bit her lip with pleased anticipation as she placed her hands on Jack's broad shoulders. She did like when Jack kissed her. It always sent butterflies fluttering in her stomach and made her feel warm and secure.

Winking at her and offering one last grin of encouragement, Jack's head began to descend toward Jilly's. She closed her eyes when he pressed his lips to hers, sighing when the now familiar fluttering sensation of delight began in her stomach. Jilly slipped her arms around Jack's neck when he pulled her against him, wrapping his arms around her waist and kissing her again.

"You're the sweetest girl in Mourning Dove Creek, you know?" Jack mumbled as he paused in kissing Jilly a moment.

Jilly smiled. "And you're the handsomest man in Mourning Dove Creek, you know," she flirted in return.

Jack smiled. "I *do* know," he said.

Jilly giggled. Jack Taylor was so predictable—and a little conceited. He really did think he was the handsomest man in Mourning Dove—and he was, for the most part.

Secretly, however, if Jilly ever allowed herself

to be completely honest about it (which she tried to avoid), there was one other man in Mourning Dove who always crossed her mind when the subject of the handsomest man in town arose. Yet there was no lingering on thinking of *that* man—no sirree! Not for a moment! Not for any reason—ever. And so Jilly just kept telling Jack that he was the handsomest man in Mourning Dove Creek. Besides, it was almost true—being that the other man lived outside of town and not right in town the way Jack did.

And so, as Jilly Adams stood in the lovely little grove of dogwoods, sparking with the second-most handsome man in Mourning Dove Creek, she felt very near completely content. The day was bright with warm sunshine, and the scent of wildflowers perfumed the air. In fact, as Jack unexpectedly tightened his embrace around her, she felt the bouquet of flowers she'd been holding in one fist at his back tumble from her hand. But she didn't have much time to really consider that she'd dropped the flowers, for all at once, Jack's kiss intensified with an unfamiliar force.

All at once, the fluttering sensation in Jilly's stomach gave way to something else—a moment of uncertainty—quickly followed, however, by a strong desire to allow Jack to kiss her with his lips parted the way he'd begun to.

Had it not been for the sound of distant screaming, Jilly might have remained locked in

Jack's arms as his kisses grew moist and hot. But she found herself rather unexpectedly relieved when the screams and shouts for help drew closer, causing Jack to release her and both of them to look upstream from whence the sounds were coming.

"Help! Help!" a woman was crying as she ran toward them. A man was close at her heels, also shouting for help.

"What on earth?" Jack said as he and Jilly stepped from the grove of dogwoods.

"That looks like Mrs. Lillingston," Jilly said. An unhappy feeling of dread began to rise in Jilly's bosom.

"And Mr. Lillingston too," Jack said.

"Jack!" Mr. Lillingston shouted. "In the crick! He's in the crick! Catch him!"

"What?" Jack called.

But Jilly understood at once! Racing to the swollen creek bank, Jilly looked to the water in time to see a small red wooden bucket being tossed on the surface of the racing creek. Normally the creek simply babbled along at a nice, slow pace. But the rain in the mountains had turned Mourning Dove Creek into a small and rather violent river. As swift creek waters tossed the little wooden bucket as it carried it away, somehow Jilly knew what would come next.

"Georgie fell into the crick upstream!" Mr. Lillingston hollered. "We can't catch up with him! Pull him out when he gets to you, Jack! You've got to pull him out!"

Instantly, Jack was running, not upstream but downstream—and Jilly knew why. Mourning Dove Creek emptied into Mourning Dove Pond, and Mourning Dove Pond emptied into the Arkansas River by way of a series of waterfalls. If little Georgie Lillingston wasn't pulled out of the creek or pond before the waterfalls, he'd be lost over the falls to perish in the raging river below!

It was then that Jilly looked to see the small dark head of a child bobbing up and down in the water as it raced toward her. Glancing around, she could see then that there was no way to get to the boy from where she stood. Too many rocks and bushes that were normally above the water line were now beneath it. Jack had run ahead to find a better venue into the creek.

Mrs. Lillingston had already stumbled and fallen, and although she was once more on her feet and running, she was now far behind her husband. Furthermore, Georgie's position in the creek was far ahead of Mr. Lillingston's on the bank. There was no conceivable way the boy's father would ever catch him.

Without further thought, Jilly turned and began running downstream as fast as she could. She and Jack were Georgie's only hope of rescue, and as she ran, she tried not to think of her parents—

of their fatal plunge into the same river that the creek now swept little Georgie Lillingston toward.

"Come on, Jack!" Jilly panted as she saw Jack quickly wade out into the creek. She gasped as she saw the force of the rushing water unbalance him, being that it was up to his chest. "Jack!" she called, frantic. But then she saw him reach up and take hold of a large tree limb that was hanging out over the creek. Holding onto the tree limb with one hand, Jack positioned himself as close to the center of the raging creek as he could without getting swept into the current.

But still Jilly ran—for she knew that if Jack failed to latch onto Georgie, she would be the little boy's last hope. And so she ran—ran as fast as she could—panting so hard her own breath sounded like the chugging of a steam engine crossing a bridge. For a moment, Jilly imagined she could hear the train racing along over the gorge bridge so many years before—thought she heard the screams of its passengers as the railway bridge began to crumble, sending them plummeting to their deaths in the river below.

Yet still she ran—running for Georgie Lillingston's life!

CHAPTER TWO

As she ran—her lungs burning and her legs weakening—Jilly was conscious of how far upstream the Lillingston place was. No doubt Mr. and Mrs. Lillingston had been running the entire distance. It was already a miracle that their endurance had lasted this long.

Reaching an area on the creek bank that looked like a viable place to wade in, Jilly stopped running and turned to see if the little Lillingston boy had reached Jack's location yet.

"He's almost to you, Jack!" Mr. Lillingston shouted, collapsing to his knees for a moment. "Get him! Please get him, Jack!"

Jilly startled with a sudden jolt of being surprised as a bay horse abruptly reined in beside her. She'd been so intent on watching the terrible situation with Georgie Lillingston unfold before her that she hadn't heard the horse until it was right upon her.

"You stay out of that water, girl!" the man on the horse growled at her. "It won't do no good to have two children drownin' today."

Jilly looked up into the frowning, brooding,

angry expression of none other than Boone Ramsey—the farmer and cattle rancher who owned the property surrounding Mourning Dove Creek's outlet and its pond.

She had no time to respond to his rather high-handed demands, for Boone Ramsey turned his horse and rode hell-bent for the bridge that spanned the inlet where the creek emptied into the pond.

Jilly glanced to where Jack stood, wading in the raging waters of the swollen creek. She watched the little red bucket still tossing on the water's surface as it passed him.

"What do I do?" she breathed to herself. Quickly she looked to the bridge—watched as Boone Ramsey's horse trotted up onto it—watched as Boone Ramsey leapt from his saddle, over the side of the bridge, and into the pond water below.

He bobbed to the surface and swam toward the place where the stream was pouring into the pond.

"What do I do?" Jilly breathed again. She started toward the water, afraid Jack would miss catching Georgie.

"Stay there!" Mr. Ramsey shouted from his place in the pond. She watched as he seemed to struggle in the water a moment before tossing one boot over his head onto the bank of the pond and then the other. "You stay right there!" he shouted again, pointing an index finger at Jilly.

Though Jilly's mind was still uncertain as to what to do—whether to wade out into the swiftly rushing water in an attempt to help or to stay safely on the banks and pray that Jack or Mr. Ramsey were able to save the boy—it seemed her body had decided to adhere to Mr. Ramsey's demands. Thus, she watched the little red bucket leaping to and fro in the water as it passed her and headed toward the pond.

"Georgie!" she heard Jack shout. "Georgie! Grab my hand!"

"Grab his hand, Georgie," Jilly breathed as she watched the boy bobbing helplessly in the water as it pushed him toward Jack.

Jilly gasped as she saw Jack reach out and catch hold of Georgie's arm. "You've got him!" she cried out as tears filled her eyes. "You've got him!"

"Don't let go, Jack!" Mr. Lillingston hollered as he made his way downstream. "I'm almost there! Don't let him go!"

Yet at that very moment—as if the devil himself were trying to ensure Georgie's demise—a large tree branch that was also being washed downstream by the mountain rains barreled into Jack and Georgie, knocking Jack back into the water and snatching Georgie from his grasp.

"No!" Jilly screamed. "Oh no!" Looking downstream to where Boone Ramsey was still treading water in the pond, Jilly shouted, "He lost him! They're both in the water!"

"Well, you stay out of it!" Mr. Ramsey shouted.

"Jilly! Jilly!"

Jilly turned to see Jack climbing out of the creek near where she stood. But in the same instant, Georgie Lillingston was swept past her. His only hope was Boone Ramsey.

Looking to Jack, she nodded when he gestured she should run alongside the boy downstream. "Go! Go! I'm fine!" Jack panted.

Lifting her skirts, Jilly began to run once more. She didn't know what she would do, or how she could possibly help, but she ran toward the pond all the same.

"Hang on, Georgie!" she cried when she caught a glimpse of the boy's head as it broke the surface of the water. "Hang on! Mr. Ramsey will catch you!"

And all of a sudden, Jilly herself knew it was true. Even before Boone Ramsey caught hold of Georgie as the rushing creek water emptied into the pond—even before he began swimming with the little boy, holding his head above the water as they made their way to shore—Jilly knew Boone Ramsey would save Georgie Lillingston. After all, he'd done it before.

Not that Mr. Ramsey had saved Georgie from drowning before, but it seemed the ever-brooding and grumbling Boone Ramsey was always saving someone from something—always keeping someone from getting trampled by a team of horses or climbing down a cliff to help someone who had fallen and broken a limb—always. Boone Ramsey was Mourning Dove Creek's assumed hero—though he did not like to be thanked and more often than not growled at anyone who did thank him. Therefore, Jilly had indeed known he would be successful in catching Georgie before he reached the falls and the river below—even before he'd done it.

"He ain't breathin'," Mr. Ramsey panted as Jilly reached the bank of the pond in time to help him pull Georgie out. "Get him on his side," the bossy farmer ordered.

Still, Jilly did as Boone Ramsey instructed, turning Georgie on his side and patting his back.

"Here," Mr. Ramsey said as he swept back his wet hair with one hand, still careless of the water dripping from it onto his face. "Let me try," he said.

It was then that Jilly realized she was breathless as well—nearly as breathless as Georgie—breathless for the sake that she feared the little boy was already dead—breathless for the sake that she was frighteningly intimidated in the presence of Boone Ramsey.

In truth, Boone Ramsey scared the wadding out of Jilly—whether he were the handsomest man in Mourning Dove Creek or not. Most everyone in town was never sure whether to say good morning to the man when they passed him in the street or run for their lives in fear that he might chomp their heads clean off. And Jilly was no different.

The sound of Georgie coughing and spitting water from his mouth as he began to breathe again drew Jilly's attention away from Boone Ramsey and back to the little boy.

"You okay there, boy?" Mr. Ramsey asked in a kind, concerned voice.

Georgie nodded as Mr. Ramsey helped him to sit up. "D-did you g-get my bucket, mister?" the child stammered as he began to shiver.

Raking a hand back through his wet hair and exhaling a heavy sigh, Boone Ramsey answered, "I'm afraid not, boy. Sorry."

"That's all right," Georgie said. "I suppose I can get me another one someday."

"I suppose so," Mr. Ramsey agreed, an uncharacteristic chuckle rumbling in his throat.

Jack arrived, dropping to his knees beside Jilly. "You okay, Georgie?" he asked. "Sorry I lost you back there. That big ol' tree limb about did us in, didn't it?"

"Yes, sir," Georgie agreed as Jack tousled his hair.

"Good catch there, Boone," Jack said to Mr. Ramsey then.

"Yep," was all the standoffish man said as he rose to his feet.

"Georgie! Oh, my baby!" Mrs. Lillingston sobbed, dropping to her knees and gathering Georgie into her arms.

"Thank you, Boone," Mr. Lillingston panted, offering a hand to the grumbling hero. "I don't know how I can ever repay you."

"No need," Boone said, shaking the man's hand once firmly before rather staggering toward his boots that lay soaking but safe on the grass nearby.

"And you too, Jack," Mr. Lillingston said, shaking Jack's hand. Then Mr. Lillingston looked to Jilly. "I was a might worried that you were contemplatin' jumpin' into the creek after Georgie yourself, Jilly," he said, smiling at her—though he still wore a worried expression.

"W-well . . . I was," Jilly admitted, "until Mr. Ramsey arrived and I thought better of it."

"You best get that boy in to see Doc Havasham, Abe," Boone Ramsey said as he pulled on his boots. "That water in his lungs . . . could cause some problems if the doc ain't in on it."

"Of course," Mr. Lillingston agreed. "Of course. And thank you again, Boone. I know that if you hadn't been here . . . hadn't gone in after him . . . "

"Doc Havasham will know what to watch for," Boone Ramsey interrupted, however. Looking to where his horse still stood obediently on the bridge, Mr. Ramsey whistled through his teeth, and the horse immediately began walking to meet him. Once the horse had reached him, Boone Ramsey simply climbed into his saddle, nodded to Georgie and the rest of them, said, "Have a good afternoon, folks," and rode away.

"And then he just rode off," Jilly explained. "He just rode off . . . as if nothin' so awful had even happened."

Doolin Adams chuckled. "I'm not surprised. Not at all," he said. "Seems it's always the way with Boone, ain't it, Effie?" he asked his wife.

Effie Adams nodded. "Yep. When it comes to communicatin' . . . that man seems to hold to the opinion that a body oughta use as few words as possible."

"Seems to me he'd rather just shake his head or nod instead of speakin' at all if he can manage it," Doolin added.

"And is Georgie all right then, Jilly?" Effie asked her granddaughter.

Jilly shrugged. "He seems to be," she answered, "though Mr. and Mrs. Lillingston were on their way to see Doc Havasham when Jack and I left them. Mr. Ramsey said the water in his lungs might pose a problem."

Jilly's grandpa exhaled a heavy sigh, shaking

his head with relief. "They're lucky they didn't lose him over the falls," he said.

Then, wagging a scolding index finger at Jilly, her grandmother added, "And you're lucky you didn't step foot in that creek, Jilly Adams. I woulda tanned your hide if you would've drowned tryin' to help save that boy."

Jilly smiled as she glanced to her grandpa and saw him wink at her. She knew her Grandpa Doolin was thinking the same thing she was—that being, if Jilly had drowned, would her Grandma Effie have really felt like tanning Jilly's hide?

"I'm just glad that Boone Ramsey was at hand again," Effie said, picking up her knitting needles and yarn and starting her rocking chair to a rhythmic rocking as she began to knit once more. "I swear, that boy is always pulling somebody out of somethin'. Seems half the town would be dead or destitute if it weren't for him."

"And how was your walk with Jack, Jilly?" her grandpa asked, abruptly changing the subject. "I mean, other than the near tragedy with the Lillingston boy and all?"

Jilly smiled. In truth, it always rattled her a little of late—the way her grandpa would suddenly change venue of a conversation subject without an obvious reason. It seemed to Jilly that this behavior was becoming more frequent. But she just tallied it up to the fact that her Grandpa

Doolin and Grandma Effie were growing older. They had both slowed down considerably over the past couple of years. After all, they were, in truth, Jilly's great-grandparents, and far older than any other folks in Mourning Dove Creek. It made a certain amount of sense to Jilly that older folks nearing their eighties might need a little more rest—might have trouble remembering things now and again.

Therefore, Jilly just smiled at her grandpa and answered, "It was right nice, Grandpa," she said. Blushing, she added, "Walks with Jack are always nice."

"Sparkin' tends to make that the case," her grandpa chuckled.

"Doolin!" Effie scolded. "Don't you go encouragin' her now."

"What?" Doolin asked, however. "It ain't like you and I didn't sneak off for a bit of sparkin' now and again when we were courtin', Effie."

"That was different," Effie contended. "You had already asked for my hand in marriage. And anyway, my father would've lopped off your head and set you on fire if he'd ever have found out."

"Oh, but things are different now days," Doolin reminded her. "Most folks are plum near to heathens now . . . especially west of the Mississippi."

"Well, that doesn't make it all right," Effie

argued. She plopped her knitting down in her lap, stopped the rhythmic rocking of her chair, and leaned toward Jilly. "Don't you go lettin' that Taylor boy grope you all over or anything the like, Jilly. I can tolerate a minimal amount of sparkin' here and there . . . but you be sure that's all it comes to. Do you understand me?"

Jilly rolled her eyes. "Of course, Grandma." Then shrugging her shoulders and frowning a bit, she asked, "And besides . . . what else is there?"

The laughter that erupted from her Grandpa Doolin sent his top set of false teeth tumbling out of his mouth and into his lap. Jilly giggled, entirely amused as she watched him fumble with the piece of vulcanized rubber securing porcelain teeth, as he tried to insert them back into his mouth even as he continued to laugh.

"Oh, for Pete's sake, Doolin!" Effie scolded. "Get that thing back in your mouth where it belongs! Nothin' in all the world is that funny!"

But as her grandpa continued to laugh—mirth causing his faded blue eyes to water—Jilly continued to giggle. Oh, how she adored the loving banter between her grandma and grandpa—the way her Grandma Effie pretended to be so astonished and aghast at her grandpa's behavior, the way her Grandpa Doolin intentionally provoked his wife into scolding him.

She watched a moment, not really hearing their words as they playfully bantered back and forth—just watched, studied the merriment in their eyes, the loving winks they exchanged. Jilly watched as her grandma returned to her knitting, gently pushing on the floor with her feet to cause her rocking chair to begin rhythmically rocking again. She watched as her grandpa retrieved his pipe from the small table near his own chair and stuffed it with the sweet-smelling tobacco he kept in a small pouch in his trousers pocket. She saw her grandma scold him as he struck a match on his pant leg and began to puff on his pipe to ensure the tobacco lit.

For a moment, Jilly closed her eyes and listened—listened to the calming sound of the familiar squeak her grandma's rocker made when she was sitting in it. She inhaled the sweet, comforting aroma of pipe smoke as her grandpa puffed. It was a warm evening, and the crickets had begun to chirp outside, and Jilly's stomach was still full and satisfied from a delicious supper of smoked ham and buttered biscuits.

"What you thinkin' about, Jilly honey?" her grandma asked.

Though her tranquil moment of reflection had been interrupted by her grandma's question, Jilly didn't mind, for her grandma's sweet voice was part of her comfort—part of all that made Jilly feel safe and secure, loved and cared for.

"She's thinkin' about all them sweet kisses Jack Taylor give her this afternoon before the

Lillingston boy almost drowned. Ain't you, pumpkin?" her grandpa teased.

"Oh, she is not," her grandma argued. Looking to Jilly then, she continued, "I don't like that Jack Taylor, Jilly. He seems all too flirtatious and such to me. Why don't you let some nice, reasonable, steady young man court you a bit? You know, someone like that handsome Clarence Farley. He seems to be a very steady, capable young man."

"Clarence Farley?" Jilly heard her grandpa exclaim in unison with her.

"Clarence Farley?" her grandpa nearly hollered. "Why, that boy is as ugly as a mud fence!"

"Now, Doolin, that is not true," Effie contended. "Clarence might not be as handsome as Jack Taylor, Boone Ramsey, or even Daniel McDonald . . . but he has a very sweet countenance, and he's very polite."

"And he sits in Sunday services pickin' his nose like he expects to find a gold nugget up in there or somethin'," Doolin mumbled.

"Oh, he does not," Effie argued, though only halfheartedly and through her own giggling.

"He does, Grandma," Jilly added. Wrinkling her nose, she added, "I could never like a man who picks his nose the way poor Clarence does."

"Well, honey, all men pick their noses," Effie pointed out.

"Well, that may be," Jilly admitted. "But I've never seen another man do it the way Clarence

Farley does. In fact, I'm not sure I've ever seen anyone over the age of four years pick their nose, at least in public, and—"

"All right, all right," Effie sighed. "Poor Clarence Farley is out of the runnin', I guess." Speeding up the rhythm of her rocker, she added, "Now I'll never be able to look at that boy again without hopin' he doesn't want to shake my hand." As her rocker stopped rocking altogether then, Effie plopped her knitting down in her lap as her eyes widened. "Oh mercy! I just remembered . . . Clarence Farley served me a piece of peach pie at the last town social." Gasping, she continued, "Do you think he washed his hands before slicin' it for me?"

Jilly watched as her grandpa began to choke on his pipe smoke and laughter—as he clamped his hand over his mouth to keep his false teeth from dropping into his lap again.

She wondered if other families in Mourning Dove Creek were as entertaining to converse with as hers was. She thought not and felt sorry for them. After all, what was life if not for the happy times spent with loved ones—whether friends or family, whether parents or grandparents?

Jilly sighed, suddenly even more thankful that the little Lillingston boy had been saved. Though she was certain Mr. and Mrs. Lillingston and their other children were still very emotional and entirely rattled at what had happened with

Georgie, now she was even more grateful that he had not been lost—that Boone Ramsey had managed to catch hold of him as he emptied into the pond with the rushing creek water.

She was also thankful that she'd had her Grandpa Doolin and Grandma Effie to go to when her parents had been taken by tragedy—so very, very thankful. After all, what would've happened to her if she hadn't had them? Jilly again thought of Boone Ramsey, for his past held loss and tragedy very much like her own—and she felt sorry for him. For as she sat there in the warm, loving companionship and protection of her grandparents' company and home, she knew that, after Georgie Lillingston had been saved that day, Boone Ramsey returned home to an empty house and no one.

"Lane O'Hara then," Jilly heard her grandma say.

"Lane O'Hara?" her grandpa exclaimed with disgust. "Why, he's as old as Methuselah, Effie!"

"Now don't be ridiculous, Doolin," Effie lovingly quibbled. "No one is as old as Methuselah, and you know it."

Jilly giggled as she watched her grandpa return to puffing on his pipe. He winked at her and grinned—letting her know that getting her grandma's goat was still his favorite pastime in life.

She studied them for a moment longer—the top

of her grandpa's shiny, bald head and the tufts of white hair lingering above his ears, his faded but still smiling blue eyes and ruggedly bronzed and leathered skin. Her grandma was as beautiful as ever with her white hair piled so perfectly, her green eyes glistening with love and contentment, and her rather gnarled-by-life fingers expertly working her knitting.

"How about I choose for myself?" Jilly interjected then. "And I choose Jack Taylor."

"How about you don't worry about choosin' right now, Jilly honey?" Effie said, smiling at her. "Why don't you worry about knockin' some sense into your grandpa's thick head instead?"

"My head ain't any thicker than yours, Effie my girl," Doolin said, smiling at his wife.

Jilly sighed and sat back in her own chair. She wondered if there were still a biscuit left she could slather with some of her grandma's strawberry preserves. She figured that if there were, her life would be perfectly flawless in that warm, comforting moment. Yes—perfectly flawless.

CHAPTER THREE

Boone Ramsey waited until dark to make his way to Doc Havasham's place. He'd fretted over the well-being of the Lillingston boy all through the remainder of the day. Yet if there were one thing Boone Ramsey didn't like, it was attention, and stopping in at Doc Havasham's to inquire of the boy's condition during daylight hours certainly would've drawn attention. So he'd waited—waited until the sun set and the supper hour had most likely passed at the Havasham home.

Boone hoped the Lillingston boy was well—hoped the creek water in his lungs hadn't damaged him permanently. He was just glad he'd been riding out to check on a line of fence he'd repaired the day before, heard the hollering, and been able to assist in getting the boy out of the water. He didn't want to imagine the pain the Lillingstons would've been enduring had their son been lost over the falls. Not that he couldn't imagine the pain; in truth, he could. He just didn't want to.

As Boone stepped up on the boardwalk,

Clarence Farley passed him, nodded, and said, "Evenin', Boone."

"Evenin'," Boone managed in response. He frowned, wondering why folks were still milling around outside at such an hour. Yet it was a warm summer night, so no doubt more folks than usual felt like socializing.

Boone lifted his right arm a bit to stretch out his sore shoulder. Grabbing hold of the Lillingston boy and swimming to shore had aggravated it a bit. He was well aware of the stitches Doc Havasham had put in the laceration on his back the day before as well. No doubt the goings-on down at the creek and pond had irritated the stitches at his back a bit too. But he figured they'd hang on as long as they needed to. Truth was, Boone was annoyed that he'd even had to have Doc sew up the wound in the first place. But try has he might, he'd known as soon as the ax had fallen off the barn wall and cut him that there was no way he could reach around to sew the laceration up himself the way he usually did when he was cut. So he'd gone to Doc Havasham and had him do it.

Boone shook his head—unable to remember another time in his entire life that he'd been to see a doctor two days in a row. Of course, this time it wasn't for any care for himself—just to inquire after the Lillingston boy.

He heard voices as he approached the doc's

house—saw that the side door leading to the doc's workplace stood open, allowing the orange glow of an evening lamplight to cast shadows on the boardwalk. Feeling less like being social than he had even a moment before, Boone stepped off the boardwalk and around to sit on a bench that had been placed just alongside one wall of the house.

Taking a seat in order to wait until Doc Havasham was finished with his current patient, Boone realized that the calm of the night allowed him to hear the conversation passing between Doc Havasham and the man he was speaking to. As he listened to what was being said, Boone figured it wasn't his fault he could hear them. What was he supposed to do, shove a finger in each ear to keep from eavesdropping? Yet even as he silently scolded himself for listening so intently to the conversation between the two men, Boone's ears perked up when he realized that the man Doc was talking with was Doolin Adams.

Doolin Adams was most likely the best man in Mourning Dove Creek—and also the oldest. He was a man to be admired—hard-working, honest, and kind. Yet he didn't put up with any guff—none—especially when it came to his granddaughter, Jilly. In fact, in that moment, Boone wondered why in the world a man like Doolin was allowing his granddaughter to keep company with the likes of Jack Taylor. Jack was good-looking enough to have all the female hearts in Mourning Dove Creek fluttering like hummingbird wings, but he was a real tomcat, and Boone thought that maybe Doolin's near eighty-year-old mind might not be as sharp as it once was when it came to looking out for his granddaughter.

And then Boone wondered for a moment if he owned some sort of mysterious powers of the mind—for the very next words out of Doolin Adams's mouth were, "I don't know, Joe. That damn Taylor boy seems to have his hooks dug deep into my Jilly. If I make it long enough, I know I can wrangle her away from him, help her see what he's really made of. But now that you're tellin' me my lungs and heart are so much worse . . . what if I head onto the roundup in heaven before she's settled with a good man?"

"If you want my advice as not only a doctor but also a father . . . don't wait on it, Doolin," Doc Havasham counseled. "Jack Taylor has his eye on Jilly . . . today. But he'll move on soon enough. My Dina learned that the hard way, so don't let your Jilly fall victim to his ways. If I were you, I'd see she was settled in with a good man before . . . well, before you go." Doc Havasham paused and then added, "If it helps at all, I happen to know that Clarence Farley is sweeter than sugar on Jilly. Why not see if you can drive her toward Clarence and away from

Jack? Clarence . . . he's a good young man."

"Nope," Doolin sighed, however. "He's got some . . . some habits Jilly finds . . . well, downright unacceptable. Nope, if I had my druthers and was able to choose for Jilly myself, it would be . . . well . . . it wouldn't be Jack Taylor, that's for sure."

"Well, I don't mean to be bringin' your spirits down, Doolin," Doc Havasham began. "But you best see to gettin' things in order . . . especially where Effie and Jilly are concerned. All right?"

"I hear ya," Doolin sighed. "Well, you have a good evenin', Joe. Say hello to Verna for me."

"I will, Doolin. Same to Effie," Doc Havasham called as Doolin Adams stepped out onto the boardwalk and headed home.

Boone watched the old man walk away into the warm dark of a summer's night. The elderly man had quite a quick step for his age. Yet the conversation Boone overheard between Doolin and Doc Havasham left Boone wiser than he had been a few moments before. Doolin Adams was wearing out. Furthermore, Boone understood Doolin's concern about his granddaughter and her choice of beau.

Still, it wasn't any of his nevermind. So he stood from his place on the bench and hurried to Doc Havasham's still-open door.

"Hey there, Doc," Boone greeted. He could tell that Doc Havasham had been watching Doolin

Adams saunter away into the night as well, and his expression of concern and defeat told him that Doolin didn't have many more sauntering days left.

"Oh, hey there, Boone," the doctor greeted, forcing a welcoming smile.

"Sorry to bother you so late, Doc," Boone began, "but I wanted to see if you'd had a chance to look over the Lillingston boy today . . . assumin' you heard what happened to him and all."

Doc Havasham nodded. "I did indeed, Boone," he answered. "And I thank you for encouragin' Abe and Elly to bring him in. We do need to be watchin' over him, bein' that old pond water got into him the way it did."

"But you think he'll be fine and all?" Boone asked, still concerned.

Doc nodded again. "I do. He seems right as rain to me. Thanks to you."

Boone shook his head. "No. I just happened to be there," Boone mumbled.

"The way you always do, hmmm?" Doc asked, grinning with understanding. He frowned a moment then, asking, "And how's that nasty gash on your shoulder doin' today?"

Boone shrugged. "Well enough, I suppose. I haven't thought much of it."

But as Doc Havasham drew in a discouraged breath when he leaned around and looked at the back of Boone's shirt, Boone figured he was in for more stitching.

"Yep. From the dried blood back here, I figure you tore some of those stitches helpin' that boy out today," Doc said. "You best come in and let me wash that thing out and put a couple more stitches in you."

"Oh, I'm sure it'll be fine, Doc," Boone kindly argued. "I don't want to be any more bother than I have been already."

"Come on in, Boone," Doc ordered, however. "Let's just make sure you don't have an infection brewin', all right?"

Reluctantly Boone stepped into the doc's office. He just wanted to get on home. He'd only come to check up on the Lillingston boy, and now he was preparing to get restitched—not to mention the fact that his mind was lingering on poor Doolin Adams and his quandary over his granddaughter.

Boone thought of Jack Taylor and frowned. Somebody ought to take that flirting tomcat down, knock some sense into him where women were concerned—especially the Adams girl. The fact was, Jilly Adams owned a special place in Boone's heart—and not just because they had both been orphaned along life's path. Jilly Adams had done Boone a great service many years before, when she was just a girl. He doubted she even remembered what she'd done, but it didn't matter—because Boone did remember. And because he remembered, he'd always felt a bit more protective of Jilly Adams than was most likely normal. He found that now that he knew Doolin Adams's days were numbered, that sense of wanting to protect Jilly Adams was multiplying faster than the creek had swept the Lillingston boy away earlier in the day.

But what could he do? How could he help protect Doolin's girl when she was so kitten-eyed over the likes of Jack Taylor?

Boone flinched just a little as Doc Havasham began to add more stitches to the ones he'd put in Boone's back the day before.

"Well, it won't be a pretty scar, Boone, that's for sure," Doc said. "You sure tore this mess up savin' that Lillingston boy today."

Boone just shrugged. What was a little discomfort and another scar when compared with a boy's life? Anyway, his mind was onto other concerns. And as an idea began to form in his brain, Boone wondered if, instead of having mysterious powers of the mind the way he'd thought when he'd come upon Doc and Doolin talking the way he had, maybe he wasn't just plum going insane.

Jilly was happy—happier than she'd been in days. For one thing, she'd just seen Dina Havasham over at the general store, and Dina had assured Jilly that her father was certain Georgie Lillingston was right as rain. Knowing that Georgie wouldn't suffer any residual harm from his near drowning, coupled with the fact that Jack Taylor had just kissed her good-bye out by the Farleys' old barn before they'd parted ways, had Jilly feeling untroubled and near giddy.

As she approached the front porch of her home, however, Jilly paused—felt her smile fade and her brows wrinkle with curiosity.

Her grandpa was standing just inside the open front door, shaking hands with none other than Boone Ramsey, who stood just outside the front door. Jilly was still too far away to hear what her grandpa and Mr. Ramsey were saying to one another, but from the expressions on both their faces, it seemed their subject was not a mirthful one.

She watched as her grandpa said something, patting Boone on one shoulder with seeming encouragement. Boone nodded, and Jilly's grandpa closed the door. Boone Ramsey inhaled a deep breath before turning to leave, exhaling it soundly as he strode down the front porch steps.

Of course, being that Boone was now straight in her path, Jilly knew there would be no avoiding him. Therefore, she just started walking toward him and the front porch beyond.

But when Boone Ramsey looked up and caught sight of her, not only did Jilly's breath catch in her throat, but her feet quit moving as well—for in many ways, Boone Ramsey was simply a terrifying presence.

By far the handsomest man in town—tall, broad-shouldered, with thick brown hair that hung near to his shoulders and a week's worth of beard stubble serving to accent his perfectly straight nose and high, prominent cheekbones—it was the light-green color of Boone Ramsey's eyes seeming to bore a hole right through her that unsettled her most.

"Afternoon, Miss Adams," Boone said, nodding a bit and touching the brim of his hat as he stared at her.

"Afternoon, Mr. Ramsey," Jilly managed to respond as the intimidation the man unwittingly poured over her began to cause her insides to tremble.

"You have a good evenin'," he said as he continued to look at her—as his stride drew him nearer and nearer.

"You too," she gulped as he brushed past her then. She could've sworn her grandma's bright red geraniums were wilting with intimidation as well. But once Boone Ramsey was beyond her and at her back, Jilly found her feet and breath again and hurried up the front porch steps and into the house.

"Oh, that man scares the life out of me for some reason!" she exclaimed, closing the door behind her. "I don't remember him bein' so frightenin' before he left school."

"Who?" her grandma asked from her place in the parlor.

Striding into the parlor, Jilly answered, "Boone Ramsey." Shaking her head, she looked to her grandpa as he took a seat in his chair opposite her grandma's rocker. "And whatever was he doin' over here anyway, Grandpa? Have you got business with him that I don't know about or somethin'?"

Jilly was again unsettled when her grandpa didn't smile and say something amusing. Rather, he frowned and answered, "As a matter of fact, yes, Jilly . . . I do."

Jilly gulped as she noticed the moisture gathering in her grandmother's eyes. Moreover, her grandpa looked overly fatigued and suddenly so much older than he'd seemed that morning.

"What's wrong?" she asked as trepidation began to grow inside her.

"I've always found it's best just to say things plain and simple, Jilly," Doolin began. "And that's what I plan on doin' here. Fact is, Boone Ramsey come by today to ask my permission to marry you, Jilly . . . and I gave it to him."

"What?" Jilly gasped. "What? You're . . . you're just foolin' with me, Grandpa. I know you are. I don't know Boone Ramsey from a hole in the ground! And . . . and anyway, I'm in love with

Jack! I plan on marryin' Jack Taylor! So how can you possibly be sittin' here tellin' me that you gave Boone Ramsey permission to marry me?"

"It's best, dear," Effie said. "Boone is a good man, the best of men . . . especially in this town. He's got a successful farm and ranch, already has a house built. He'll take care of you, Jilly honey. And your grandpa and me . . . we can rest well knowin' you'll be well cared for and protected when we're gone."

"Grandpa!" Jilly cried as tears began to stream over her cheeks. "You can't mean this! You know I love Jack Taylor! You know that Boone Ramsey scares the life out of me! How could you tell him that—"

"Jack Taylor is a scoundrel, Jilly," her grandpa interrupted firmly. "He'll toy with you like a kitten does a ball of yarn and then turn around and find another girl's heart to break. Your grandma and me, we ain't gettin' any younger, honey. We have to think ahead. And I'll tell you straight right here and now . . . that if I could choose any man I've ever known to be your husband, it would be Boone Ramsey. God is watchin' over you, Jilly, because Boone come to me today, just after I spent the night prayin' about what to do where you're concerned. Boone just walked up the front porch and into the parlor and asked me for your hand, and I gave it to him . . . without one worry in my soul or heart, Jilly."

“I can’t marry a stranger, Grandpa!” Jilly sobbed, however. “I can’t!”

“Boone ain’t no stranger to you, Jilly, and you know it,” Doolin argued. “You’ve known that man since you came to Mournin’ Dove Creek to be with us, honey. He’s not a stranger to you.”

“He scares me, Grandpa,” Jilly whispered through her tears.

Doolin nodded. “I know. I know. And I suspect there’s a reason for that . . . which you’ll come to discover over time.”

But Jilly shook her head. “I won’t do it, Grandpa. I won’t. I won’t marry that awful, broodin’, unhappy man. I’m gonna marry Jack Taylor. I am.”

Doolin Adams inhaled a deep breath—and it pained his lungs. He had to remain calm and let Jilly spill out her frustrations and fears. But in the end, he knew just how obedient she was—knew that she trusted him and Effie with her life and would do whatever they counseled her to do. It might take her awhile. She might cry and fuss and even hate him for a time. But in the end, she would do what he asked; he knew she would. And so he inhaled again—remained as calm as he could while he listened to her rant on and on about how wonderful Jack Taylor was and how much he loved her.

Jack Taylor was a fool, however, and Doolin

knew it. He also agreed with what Boone Ramsey had only just told him minutes before—that Jack Taylor was nothing but a dirty old tomcat and ought to be beaten within an inch of his life for messing around with the hearts of the girls in Mourning Dove Creek.

So Doolin allowed Jilly her ranting—her pleading and her promises that she would never marry Boone Ramsey.

And then, when at last she paused a moment to wipe her tears, Doolin inhaled another painful breath and said, "I'll give you one chance, Jilly. Well . . . I guess the truth is I'll give Jack Taylor one chance. You go over to the Taylors' place right now, and you tell Jack what I've done . . . that I've agreed to let Boone Ramsey marry you. You tell Jack that, and tell him that if he wants to come over and talk me out of it . . . then I'll reconsider."

"Do you mean it, Grandpa?" Jilly asked, the fear and desperation in her eyes heartbreaking to Doolin for a moment.

"I do mean it," Doolin answered.

"Doolin!" Effie began to argue. "You already promised Boone."

But Doolin nodded and said, "I know. I know." He looked up to Jilly then. "You go tell Jack Taylor what's happened today, Jilly, and though I know what he's gonna say already . . . I think you need to hear it for yourself."

"But if I'm right," Jilly began, "if I'm right, Grandpa . . . you'll let me marry Jack and never mention Boone Ramsey's name to me again."

Doolin nodded. "Agreed. Agreed. Now you run on over to the Taylor place, Jilly. And when Jack Taylor proves to be the disappointment of a young lifetime, you come back home, and I'll tell you why I gave Boone my permission to have you."

"Boone Ramsey won't have me, Grandpa," Jilly cried with defiance. "Jack Taylor will. You wait and see."

"Go on now," Doolin said, gesturing toward the door. "You go on and see if I ain't right about Jack Taylor."

Jilly was certain she was having a nightmare! How could she possibly be awake when the circumstances were so horrid? So frightening and painful?

She thought of one last thing then. Looking to her grandma, she asked, "Do you agree with him, Grandma? Do you think Grandpa choosin' a husband for me—choosin' Boone Ramsey, of all men—do you think he's done right? Because if you don't, I know he'll listen to you in all this. Do you think I should be made to marry Boone Ramsey?"

But Jilly's heart felt as if it might shrivel up and turn to dust as her grandma looked up to her and with tear-filled eyes answered, “Unquestionably, Jilly. Unquestionably.”

A sense of betrayal the like she had never known washed over Jilly Adams in that moment. How could they? How could her grandparents do such a thing to her? And why would they do it? Why?

“Go on now, Jilly,” Doolin said again. “You go on over and talk to Jack. And then you come home, and we’ll talk about it some more. Go on now.”

“Oh, I will go!” Jilly exclaimed as fury joined the hurt growing in her heart. “I will go, and we will talk about it when I come back. We’ll talk about my weddin’ to Jack Taylor.”

In a whirl of tears and heartache, Jilly raced out through the front door and down the street toward the Taylor place. Jack would save her! She knew he would! He would never allow her to marry anyone else but him—especially not Boone Ramsey. Jack would save her. Jilly had no doubt of it—at least, not too much doubt.

CHAPTER FOUR

"Pardon me for the intrusion, Mrs. Taylor," Jilly began, trying to appear as calm as possible. "But might Jack be at home? And if so, may I speak with him just for a moment?"

"Why, of course, Jilly," Mrs. Taylor answered. It was obvious Jack's mother was unnerved a bit. After all, she'd answered the knock on the door to find Jilly still red-faced from crying—not to mention out of breath from having run all the way from her own home to Jack's. "He's just inside," Mrs. Taylor said. "Won't you come on in, Jilly?"

But Jilly forced a smile, shook her head, and declined, "No, thank you, Mrs. Taylor. Grandma is expectin' me home right quick to help start supper."

"All right," Mrs. Taylor said, smiling with concerned compassion. Turning from Jilly, Mrs. Taylor called over her shoulder, "Jack? Jack! Jilly Adams is here. She needs to speak with you for a moment."

Quick as a rabbit, Jack appeared behind his mother at the front door.

"Hey there, Jilly," he greeted, smiling at her. "What're you doin' out this way?"

"May I . . . may I speak with you a moment, Jack?" Jilly asked as tears began to well in her eyes once more.

Jack's smile instantly disappeared. "You all right, Jilly?" he asked.

Jilly nodded, forcing a smile and willing her tears not to escape her eyes—at least not yet—not with Jack's mother looking on. "Yes. I just need to speak with you. It will only take a moment."

"Well, sure, Jilly. Sure," Jack said, stepping around his mother and closing the door behind him as he left his house.

Taking Jilly by the shoulders then, he gazed at her, inquiring, "What's wrong, Jilly? Somethin's wrong. I can see it plain as day."

As tears spilled from her eyes, Jilly began, "I-I think my grandpa has lost his mind, Jack! Simply lost his mind!"

"What? Why?" Jack exclaimed in a whisper. Taking Jilly's hand, he led her from the front porch of his home and around to one side of the house. "What did he do to make you think such a thing?"

"When I left you just a while ago . . . when I came home . . ." Jilly stammered. "Well, I was comin' up to the house, and I saw Grandpa standin' on the front porch talkin' to Boone Ramsey."

"Uh huh," Jack remarked, urging her to continue.

"Well, I didn't really think much of it. But when I reached the house and went in . . ." Jilly burst into sobs then, her voice cracking with emotion as the truth of it all spilled out. "My grandpa has told Boone Ramsey that he can marry me, Jack! Marry me! Boone Ramsey! I-I can't fathom why, but he came to the house today and asked my grandpa for my hand. And Grandpa told him he could have me! Just as plain and simple as that, Jack!" She shook her head as she continued, still disbelieving that her grandpa had agreed to Boone Ramsey's proposal. "I told Grandpa and Grandma that I love you, Jack, and that I plan on marryin' you," she babbled. "But he said . . . he said Boone Ramsey was the best of men and that—"

"Hold on, Jilly," Jack interrupted her. "Hold on."

Jilly paused in her emotional recounting of what had happened just minutes before at her home. Brushing the tears from her cheeks, she tried to settle the sobs that wracked her body as she looked to Jack expectantly.

"You're tellin' me that your grandpa is marryin' you off to Boone Ramsey?" Jack asked.

Though Jilly thought she had made everything very clear, she could understand why Jack must be as astonished and horrified as she was at hearing the news. And so she answered, “Yes, Jack. My grandpa has promised Boone Ramsey my hand in marriage. And Grandpa said that if you don’t tell him different . . . that if you don’t tell him about us—about how in love we are and that I’m gonna to be marryin’ you instead—then he says he’ll keep his word to Boone Ramsey and make me marry him. So you’ve got to come with me, Jack! You’ve got to come and tell how things are with you and me. Please . . . you’ve got to come right now!”

“Now hold on, Jilly,” Jack said. “I-I don’t want to be hurtin’ your feelin’s or anything . . . but where in the world did you ever get the notion that me and you would ever be gettin’ married?”

Jilly frowned. She was certain she had misunderstood him. “What? What do you mean, Jack?”

Jack’s frown deepened. “I never planned on marryin’ you, Jilly. I . . . I like you. I like you more than any other girl in town, right now . . . but I ain’t anywhere near ready to settle down with one woman. And I sure as hell ain’t thinkin’ on gettin’ married anytime soon.”

An angry sort of panic began to swell inside Jilly. “What?” she asked in an awed whisper. “What do you mean you like me more than any other girl in town *right now?* What do you mean by tellin’ me you don’t plan on gettin’ married anytime soon? Are you sayin’ you don’t love me,

Jack? Are you sayin' that all the time we've spent together, all the times we've stood out by the creek sparkin' . . . are you sayin' you were just playin' at me, Jack?"

Jack shrugged—and it was the shrug of a coward in Jilly's eyes.

"Well, I don't know, Jilly," he mumbled almost timidly. "I like you well enough, I suppose. But I don't have it in mind to ever marry you."

"So you don't have a care that my grandpa has promised me to another man?" Jilly choked. "You don't have one worry in mind about seein' me marry up with Boone Ramsey?"

Again Jack shrugged his coward's shrug. "I don't know, Jilly," he said. "I mean, it does seem awful harsh for your grandpa to promise you to man you don't hardly know. But everyone has always said that Doolin Adams is the wisest man in town. So maybe he's just doin' what he thinks is best and—"

Jack was silenced by the sharp, stinging slap Jilly administered to one side of his face.

As he stared at her in astonished silence, Jilly cried, "You know what, Jack Taylor? I didn't listen when everyone told me you were just a flirt . . . that you were just a fickle tomcat. I stood up for you! I let you have my heart! I let you kiss me! And here you stand, provin' to me now that they were right. You are shallow! You are just a fickle tomcat!"

When Jack merely shrugged yet again, mumbling sorry, Jilly added, "And there's somethin' else you should know, Jack Taylor . . . and that is that you do not deserve me! You are not good enough for me! My grandpa was right after all, wasn't he? And at this very moment, I'd rather marry a complete stranger than to ever see your face again."

"If there's one thing I know for certain, it's that you don't need to watch over someone when they're chokin' down their humble pie," Effie said to Doolin.

"But she's been in there cryin' for near to two hours, Effie!" Doolin exclaimed in misery.

Doolin had known darn well that Jack Taylor had no intention of ever marrying Jilly—and he thanked the Lord for it. Still, he didn't like to hear his little girl in her room sobbing her heart and soul out the way she was. It broke his already weakening heart.

"I know," Effie sighed. "But she needs to cry it out. And besides, I think she's more angry and embarrassed than heartbroken, Doolin." She shook her head. "That Taylor boy makes me so mad! Somebody oughta beat the waddin' out of him."

"Oh, I'm sure someone will someday," Doolin grumbled. "I wish I had the strength to do it myself."

Effie started her rocker rocking in an attempt to appear calm. Yet Doolin knew by the way his beloved wife's hands gripped the rocker's armrests that Effie was hell and gone from being calm.

"Poor Jilly," Doolin sighed. "But I just keep tellin' myself that there's no better man anywhere to give her over to than Boone Ramsey. He'll take care of her when we're gone . . . in every way she needs takin' care of."

"I know. I do know," Effie agreed. "But I understand Jilly's feelin's as well. A young girl's dreams of romance and love don't usually include her grandpa and grandma forcin' her to marry a man she hardly knows."

"I know it," Doolin mumbled. He paused as he noticed Jilly's sobbing had softened. It no longer echoed down the hall so mournfully miserable. "Seems she's settlin' a bit," he whispered to Effie.

Effie nodded. "Yes, indeed. And she'll come out and talk to us when she's ready. Our Jilly is a good girl . . . and in her heart she trusts us. I know she does."

"I do too," Doolin said, nodding his head. "I just hope she can forgive us one day."

Jilly brushed the tears from her cheeks, dabbing at her red, swollen eyes with the damp handkerchief she held crumpled in one hand.

She hated Jack Taylor—just hated him! How could he be so unfeeling and cruel? How could he reject her the way he'd done? Jilly could easily enough admit that her grandpa had been right about Jack and his shallow character. It wasn't her grandpa's being right that had made her so angry; it was her own stupidity! She'd been totally blinded by Jack's good looks and charm, just the way Dina Havasham had been the year before. Of course, Jilly had spent the past couple of months convincing herself that Dina just hadn't been the right girl for Jack Taylor—that Jilly Adams was the right girl for him. But now, after the way he'd rejected her feelings for him and need to be rescued from an arranged marriage, she could see what a tomcat Jack really was.

Oh, she was mad—furious! Furious with Jack and furious with herself! In fact, once Jilly had returned home and raced to her room, slamming the door behind her and throwing herself on her bed to sob out her heartache, it really hadn't taken her very long to realize that it wasn't really heartache that was wracking her body with tears and trembling. It was anger and humiliation! Jack Taylor had used her, toyed with her feelings and heart, given her false impressions of what the future would be—and of what true love was.

Jilly had half a mind to marry Boone Ramsey out of pure spite. So what if Jack Taylor, the tomcat of Mourning Dove Creek, didn't want her? Boone Ramsey, the handsomest man in town and one of the most successful farmers and ranchers in the county, *did*—though, in truth, she couldn't fathom why. But nevermind the reason for Boone Ramsey's asking for Jilly's hand. The fact remained that he had, and Jilly decided then and there that she would accept his proposal. Perhaps not as eagerly, or even as willingly, as her grandpa had for her, but she would accept it. She'd marry Boone Ramsey and show Jack Taylor that he hadn't managed to break her heart the way he'd broken Dina Havasham's.

Jilly sniffled, dabbing at her eyes with the saturated hanky.

"He's a very handsome man, after all," she said aloud to herself. "Far more handsome than you, Jack Taylor." At last, Jilly had verbalized what she'd been thinking for months about Jack Taylor and Boone Ramsey. She could've paddled her own behind for championing Jack over Boone Ramsey—or any other good, honest man in town. Even Clarence Farley was true, honest, compassionate, and hard-working, even if he did own the nasty habit of picking his nose in public—for at least he did it with honesty and hard work.

Inhaling a deep breath to try to calm the sputtering breaths that were the recovery of her sobbing, Jilly stood up from her bed and retrieved a fresh handkerchief from the nearby chest of drawers.

The soft linen of the dry handkerchief felt soothing on her swollen eyes and tear-stained cheeks. Striding to the open window, Jilly closed her eyes a moment, allowing the warm summer breeze to lend refreshment to her face as well—and to her spirit.

She thought then of something she did not like to think of—something she avoided thinking of, in truth. Her grandpa and grandma were elderly. Death had fisted harsh blows to Jilly in her past, and the thought that her grandma and grandpa might someday pass away to live forever in heaven did little to comfort her. In the depths of her soul, she knew Doolin and Effie Adams would never be able to rest in peace, whether passed away or still living, if they were taxed with the worry of the well-being of their granddaughter. Jilly knew it was why her grandpa had promised her to Boone Ramsey—for she and her grandmother were always and ever first in his mind.

She realized that, from her grandpa's point of view, there could be no better man in Mourning Dove Creek for Jilly to marry. Boone Ramsey owned vast acres of land—pastures for cattle grazing, fields for farming corn and wheat. Though always brooding, Boone Ramsey was ever polite. Even that day when Jilly had come upon him leaving her home, even with all that must have been in his mind, he bid her a proper good afternoon.

And there was no doubt in anyone's mind that he was dependable, capable, and ever willing to assist. Every posse that ever rode out of Mourning Dove Creek boasted Boone Ramsey as a member. Every barn raising was attended by Boone. Every fire brigade that had ever put out any fire for anyone included Boone Ramsey.

Certainly Jack had jumped into the creek to try and save Georgie Lillingston, but Jilly frowned as she remembered the time, only weeks before, when the Ellisons' barn had caught fire in the middle of the night. Jilly's grandpa had been part of the bucket line, and so had Boone Ramsey. But Jack Taylor—Jack Taylor claimed to have slept soundly through all the ruckus, even for the truth that the Ellisons' barn was less than a quarter mile from the Taylor place.

Jilly opened her eyes, frowning. "Oh! What a fool I am!" Jilly growled to herself. "What an utter ignoramus!"

In that moment, she had more than decided to willingly marry Boone Ramsey: she was determined to! She would no longer allow his handsome good looks and towering, muscular form to intimidate her into avoiding him. She would no longer remember him as the adolescent boy whose parents had been lost to influenza the year he had been fourteen and she only eight, and she could no longer ache with empathy for his pain each time she thought of it. She would no longer ignore the fact that she had always admired Boone Ramsey—since she was a child she'd admired him. Therefore, with the shedding of her fears and all the reasons she'd concocted and fiercely owned to keep herself from thinking of Boone Ramsey as anything other than just another man in Mourning Dove Creek, Jilly marched across the room, opened the door, and hurried down the hall toward the parlor.

"Grandpa," she said as she entered the parlor to see her very weary and wilted-looking grandparents sitting in waiting for her, "you're right. Jack Taylor is not any sort of man that any woman should respect. I'm sorry I was so awful to you both before. I love you both more than anything in all the world, and I trust your judgment. So . . . so I'll marry Boone Ramsey if you think it will be best for me. I only have one condition of my own."

"And that is?" Doolin Adams asked as the color visibly began returning to his beloved, weathered cheeks.

"I want to marry him now," Jilly answered. "As soon as possible. I don't want a big, fancy weddin' and all the expense, nonsense, and waitin' that goes along with it. I want to do it while I'm still feelin' brave enough."

"Sounds good to me," Doolin sighed, smiling with relief.

But Jilly's grandma was not so easily convinced. "Oh, Jilly honey! Are you sure? A woman only gets married once . . . at least when she's a young, beautiful thing. Don't you want a pretty dress and all?"

Jilly shook her head. "No. It would seem silly to me. I hardly know Boone Ramsey. I think it would be ridiculous to put on a big weddin' under the circumstances. No. I just want the preacher to come over here in our parlor . . . and m-marry me to him. That's all. And I won't marry him until you all agree to my one condition."

"Well . . . if that's what you really want, honey," Effie reluctantly agreed.

"It is," Jilly assured her—even though she wasn't as certain as she was pretending to be.

"Well, then . . . why don't I ride on over to Boone's place this afternoon and discuss the final arrangements with him?" Doolin said as he slowly stood from his seat in his chair. "I'm sure he won't be the one to argue about keepin' things simple."

Holding back a sudden wave of tears that rose to her eyes, and tying not to panic as the realization of what she'd just agreed to do washed over her, Jilly forced a smile. Looking to her grandma, she offered, "How about I take care of supper all on my own tonight, Grandma? After all, looks like I'll be doin' my cookin' without your help from now on."

"Somebody oughta beat the beans and other stuff out of Jack Taylor," Boone grumbled.

"I know it," Doolin agreed. "But I figure someday all his hog slop will come back on him one way or the other."

Boone shook his head with amazement at how perfectly he'd read Jack Taylor's character and lack of intentions toward Jilly Adams. "I'm sorry that he hurt her though, Doolin. She didn't deserve it . . . not at all."

"Oh, I don't think she's so much hurt as angry and humiliated," Doolin explained.

Boone chuckled. "So she's agreed to marry me out of spite, is that it?"

Doolin smiled as well. "Probably. But you and I both know that won't matter in the end."

"Do we?" Boone asked as a deep frown furrowed his brow.

"Well, I do," Doolin said, placing a thankful and reassuring hand on the man's shoulder. "I thank you for what you're doin' for me and Effie, Boone . . . and especially for Jilly. I'll rest easy when my time comes knowin' she's in your care."

"Does she know, Doolin?" Boone asked then. "Does she know that your time is . . . is comin'?"

"Not yet," Doolin admitted. "I want to get her settled in safe with you first. Then I'll let her know . . . if she hasn't already figured it out. All right?"

Boone nodded—though he felt things might go easier for Jilly Adams if she thoroughly understood her grandpa's reasons for giving her away to a strange man.

"So what do you say we have ourselves a quiet little weddin' in a couple of days, hmmm?" Doolin asked with a smile and chuckle of triumph.

"You bet," Boone agreed. "I'll ride in and talk to Reverend Dryer in the mornin' . . . see if he's got the time day after tomorrow."

"All right," Doolin said with a nod. "But I do have one more thing I wanna say to you before I leave, Boone."

Boone held his breath, for he thought he knew what was coming—a lecture on how to treat a woman with patience and tenderness on her wedding night.

Instead, he was surprised when Doolin said, "I know you're the town champion, Boone . . . that somethin' in you is so good that it drives you to save everybody from everything. Even what you're doin' now—marryin' my Jilly to keep her safe and cared for—even doin' this, I know you're doin' it because you really are a true hero. But I have to say this to you, Boone. You're gonna have my Jilly as your wife, and that means you gotta watch out for yourself better. Do you hear what I'm sayin'? Before you go jumpin' into any more ponds to save little boys, before you go ridin' off with the next posse chasin' after some outlaw . . . you think twice about what you're protectin' at home now. All right?"

Boone nodded, exhaling a breath of relief that Doolin had told him what he had, instead of broaching the subject of how to treat his granddaughter on her wedding night.

"I do hear you, Doolin," Boone said. "I really do."

"Okay . . . and I mean it, Boone. You gotta start thinkin' twice before you risk your own life anymore," Doolin reiterated.

"I will," Boone assured the old man. "I will."

"Then I'll leave you to your thoughts for now, boy," Doolin said. "But you drop by our place on your way home from meetin' with Reverend Dryer tomorrow, and we'll settle everything up, all right?"

"Yep," Boone answered.

"You have a good evenin' then, Boone," Doolin said as he awkwardly mounted his horse. "We'll see you tomorrow."

Boone nodded and watched the old man ride away, admiring the manner in which he still sat a horse straight and strong, even for his age and invisible infirmities.

Removing his hat, Boone raked his fingers back through his hair. What had he done? Had he lost his ever-loving mind? Asking Doolin Adams for his granddaughter's hand in marriage?

And yet Boone secretly gloated over the fact that Jack Taylor had turned out to be just as yellow a tomcat as he'd thought he was. At least Doolin and Effie wouldn't have to worry about Jilly ending up tied to that little weasel.

"Somebody oughta beat the waddin' out of that boy one day," Boone mumbled as he pressed his hat back onto his head and headed into the house. He guessed he better straighten up a bit. Boone didn't want Jilly Adams arriving to find a dirty house and become more despairing than she no doubt already would be after marrying up with the likes of him.

CHAPTER FIVE

Jilly hadn't slept a wink the night before. After all, how could she have? Not only was she marrying a man who was nearly a complete stranger that morning, but also her grandma had had a "little talk" with Jilly before she'd retired for the night—"a little added insight to the details of the goin's-on where the birds and the bees are concerned," Effie Adams had called it. Though Jilly knew full well how babies were conceived and birthed, Effie had explained that she didn't want Jilly going into her wedding night as ignorant about "the details" as she had been when she married Doolin so many years before.

Therefore, considering that she was going to marry Boone Ramsey in the morning, coupled with her new knowledge of the intimacies between a husband and wife, Jilly stood in the parlor with her grandma, her grandpa, and Reverend Dryer, waiting for Boone Ramsey to arrive and feeling like she'd just been run over by a train.

"Well, this all came about quite suddenly, didn't it, Miss Adams?" Reverend Dryer asked, pulling Jilly's attention from her anxieties and to him.

"Oh . . . oh yes. I suppose it seems to you like it did," she stammered.

Reverend Dryer smiled. "I could've sworn it was gonna be Jack Taylor we'd be waitin' on today."

"Oh, quit your fishin' for gossip, Reverend," Effie teased. "You know that silly Jack Taylor doesn't have a well-meanin' bone in his body." Effie put her arm around Jilly's shoulders, smiling with pride. "And our Jilly . . . why, she's just the smartest girl in town, acceptin' a proposal of marriage from Boone Ramsey the way she did. He's a prize turkey if I ever saw one."

Reverend Dryer chuckled. "Well, that does seem to be the general opinion among the ladies in Mourning Dove—accordin' to my own daughters, that is," he said. "Why, they were just plum disappointed when Boone showed up on our doorstep tellin' me Jilly had accepted his marriage proposal and askin' me to perform the ceremony." Reverend Dryer removed his pocket watch from his vest pocket. "I suppose Boone oughta be along any moment now," he mumbled as he checked the time on the face of his watch.

"I'm sure he will," Doolin said. "He probably had a mess of things he wanted to tidy up before bringin' a new wife home this afternoon."

Jilly's knees weakened, and she thought for a

moment that she might faint. It wasn't so much the reverend's obvious doubt that Boone Ramsey would really arrive and marry Jilly. It was her own doubt—and the sudden realization that she'd be going home with Boone if he did show up and marry her—going home with him to live with him—forever!

Everyone in the parlor startled at the knock on the front door. And Jilly didn't know whether she felt relief or terror when her grandpa opened it to reveal a stunningly polished-up Boone Ramsey.

"Afternoon there, Boone," Doolin said as he stepped aside and gestured for the handsome bridegroom to enter.

"Afternoon, Mr. Adams," Boone greeted as he crossed the threshold and strode into the parlor. He nodded to Jilly's grandma and said, "Mrs. Adams," in greeting. Then he looked to Reverend Dryer, offering, "Reverend."

Boone looked to Jilly last—and when he did, she could've sworn her heart reined to an abrupt halt in her chest. He was so incredibly handsome that the sight of him had taken her breath away.

It wasn't so much that he'd really changed at all since she'd seen him the day before. He was clean-shaven, and he wasn't wearing a hat the way he normally did, but he seemed almost imaginary in the power of his presence and attractive appearance. The only reason Jilly could fathom for seeing Boone Ramsey so much more as he really was was the fact that she was really, really looking at him—meeting his gaze for the first time in years—really, really staring into his fascinating light-green eyes and allowing herself to consciously admit just how powerfully drawn she was to him physically.

"Miss Adams," Boone greeted Jilly at last.

"M-Mr. Ramsey," she managed in return.

"Oh, now there's no need to be so formal," Reverend Dryer chuckled. "Shall we begin?"

"Yes," Boone answered firmly.

"Now, when I spoke with Boone yesterday, Miss Adams," Reverend Dryer began, "he assured me that it was your wish that the ceremony be not only very private but without any pomp and circumstance."

Jilly nodded. "Yes," she assured the reverend.

"Then, both of you, please face me."

Jilly did as the reverend instructed, gulped the lump of trepidation and fear that had formed in her throat, and looked up to the Reverend Dryer. She focused her attention on the small brown mole located just above the reverend's left eyebrow—commanding her knees to not give way under the weight of her anxieties.

"Boone, please take Jilly's hand," Reverend Dryer instructed.

Jilly held her breath. Would Boone Ramsey go through with marrying her? Would she go through with marrying him? *Could* she?

Yet the moment she felt Boone take her hand—firmly and without pause—something inside her leapt with . . . was it excitement? Delight? Or was it fear? Jilly could hardly tell which. But what she did know was that she liked the feel of Boone Ramsey's touch—of his warm, callused hand holding hers with such forthright confidence.

"Do you, Boone Ramsey, take Jilly Adams to be your lawful, wedded wife?" Reverend Dryer began.

"I do," Boone said—again firmly and without pause.

"And do you, Jilly Adams, take Boone Ramsey to be your husband?" the reverend continued.

"I do," Jilly heard herself answer—firmly and without pause. The determination in her own voice rather astonished her.

"Boone, your ring please," the reverend said to Boone.

Jilly frowned, for she hadn't expected to receive a ring. She watched, somewhat mystified, as Boone reached into his vest pocket and produced a beautifully ornate gold band.

"Repeat after me, Boone. With this ring, I thee wed," Reverend Dryer instructed.

Jilly's hand began to tremble as Boone raised her hand a bit and began to slip the beautiful gold band onto her left ring finger. "With this ring, I thee wed."

"Jilly, do you have a ring to give to Boone?" Reverend Dryer asked.

Jilly felt the color drain from her face. Of course she didn't have a ring! She'd only been engaged less than forty-eight hours!

"I have it," Boone said, however. Reaching into his vest pocket again, he removed a larger, somewhat worn-looking gold band.

Offering it to Jilly, he said, "It was my father's. I hope you don't mind."

"No . . . not at all," Jilly breathed as she accepted the ring.

"Jilly, repeat after me. With this ring, I thee wed," Reverend Dryer instructed.

With her hands trembling so violently she could hardly hold onto the ring, let alone push it onto Boone's finger when he held his hand out toward her, Jilly said, "With this ring . . . I thee wed."

Once she'd finally managed to get the ring onto Boone's finger, she exhaled a quiet sigh of relief. It had been a taxing task for a girl so emotionally anxious.

"Well then, I will simply say . . . I pronounce you man and wife," Reverend Dryer finished. Smiling at Jilly and then Boone, he added, "You may kiss your bride, Mr. Ramsey."

Kiss the bride? Kiss the bride? Jilly wondered what Reverend Dryer was thinking.

Yet before Jilly had even one more moment to digest what the reverend had said, or to think of something to say or do in response, Boone Ramsey took her face between his warm, strong, callused hands.

"Why, thank you, Reverend," Boone mumbled as the allure of his brilliant green eyes captured Jilly's gaze.

The kiss Boone Ramsey pressed to Jilly's lips wasn't coarse or forceful, but it wasn't polite or timid either. Rather, it was soft and moist—warm and alluring—like nothing Jilly had ever experienced before—nothing. In fact, if Jack Taylor's kisses had once caused butterflies to rise in Jilly's stomach, then by comparison several flocks of falcons simultaneously took flight in her stomach at the sense of Boone Ramsey's kiss!

It was not a long kiss, lasting no more than a few seconds. But it left Jilly breathless, dizzy, and wishing it had lasted oh-so-much longer.

As Jilly's eyes fluttered open to find Boone still gazing at her, she felt a blush rise to her cheeks as a conquering grin tugged at one corner of his mouth. He knew he'd affected her far beyond anything else ever had, and Jilly's blush deepened.

"You have my congratulations, Mr. and Mrs. Ramsey," Reverend Dryer offered, smiling as if the entire situation were solely his doing.

When neither Jilly nor Boone responded—for Jilly was still held in some kind of bewitching trance by his gaze and Boone was still holding her there—it was Jilly's grandpa who said, "Thank you, Reverend."

"Yes, thank you, Reverend Dryer," Effie added.

"And with no reception or weddin' supper to have to attend, I suppose you two will be on your way now, won't you?" Reverend Dryer asked, still smiling and looking to Jilly and Boone expectantly.

"I 'spose so," Boone said.

Jilly gasped as he suddenly swooped her up into his arms, turned, and headed for the front door.

"But . . . but . . ." she stammered in a whisper.

"Lingerin' any longer will only make you more upset than you already are, darlin'," Boone told her. "Now smile and wave to your granny. You'll most likely be seein' her tomorrow anyway."

Feeling as if she were walking in a dream, instead of being carried out of the house by her handsome new husband, Jilly forced a smile and waved to her grandpa and grandma.

They waved in return, and Boone Ramsey chuckled when Effie Adams awkwardly called, "Have fun, honey!"

Boone had brought his wagon and team, being that Jilly needed to bring a trunk full of her things with her. With little to no effort, he lifted her up onto the wagon seat and then climbed up and over her to sit next to her.

Taking the lines to the team in hand, he clicked

his tongue, and the team started forward. Jilly grabbed hold of the handle on the seat to steady herself as the wagon lurched.

She looked back over her shoulder, waving to her grandma and grandpa as they stood on the porch watching her leave. Jilly was terrified! What had she done?

"Well, that was fairly painless, wasn't it?" Boone asked.

"I-I guess so," Jilly stammered.

He frowned. "Why don't you talk a bit? It might settle your nerves some."

"I-I wouldn't know what to say," she admitted.

Boone seemed thoughtful for a moment and then suggested, "Why don't you start out by tellin' me how ol' Jack Taylor took the news that your grandpa was sellin' your soul to the devil? Hmmm?"

"I hardly think Grandpa sold my soul to the devil, Mr. Ramsey," Jilly countered, mildly amused by his dramatics.

"Best be callin' me Boone from now on . . . wife," he said.

"Well, then maybe you best be callin' me Jilly," she offered.

Boone nodded. "All righty then . . . Jilly . . . why don't you tell me how your beau took the news that I'd asked your grandpa for your hand and he'd agreed?"

Jilly frowned. Her sense of terror was subsiding

a bit. After all, Boone seemed pleasant enough at the moment. But it was the thought of Jack Taylor that kept her brow furrowed.

"I'd rather not talk about him," she mumbled.

"Because he broke your heart?" Boone inquired, kindly.

"No . . . and he didn't," she admitted.

"Because he's a jackass then?" Boone asked.

"Boone Ramsey!" Jilly exclaimed—though her frown disappeared and she had to fight the urge to giggle and smile. "That is not appropriate language!"

But Boone only shrugged.

"Why not?" Boone asked. "All a jackass is is a male donkey. In fact, I own two jackasses myself. I bought them a couple of years back. Named them Nester and Pedro."

"Yes . . . but you called Jack Taylor a . . . a . . . a male donkey," Jilly pointed out.

"That's because he's a jackass," Boone reiterated. "Jack the Jackass. I've been callin' him that in my head since I was a kid."

Jilly couldn't help herself then, for in truth the entire conversation was amusing—whether or not Boone's choice of words were proper—and she allowed a giggle to escape her throat.

"Well, you shouldn't call him that, you know . . . at least not out loud," Jilly reminded Boone.

"And you shouldn't be laughin' at it," Boone

said, looking at her and smiling. "But it don't change anything. So how did Jack the Jackass react when you told him your grandpa had promised your hand to me?"

Jilly was quiet for a moment—thoughtful. If there was one thing she'd learned in observing her grandpa and grandma, it was that there should always be pure honesty between a husband and wife. She figured that just because her marriage to Boone had been arranged instead of happening out of a natural desire to be bound to one another, it didn't change the fact that there should always be complete honesty between them.

And so with pure, however humiliating, honesty, she answered, "I think he was very glad about it . . . relieved. Now he can move onto some other idiot girl like me, who doesn't have the sense God gave a flea."

Boone exhaled what sounded to be a sigh of being perturbed and then said, "There's a big difference between bein' an idiot and bein' innocent and trusting."

Jilly grinned. "You're tryin' to make me feel better, that's all."

"Nope. It's true," he assured her. "But now you know why I've always called him Jack the Jackass."

"Because he is one," Jilly giggled.

"Always has been," Boone added, smiling at her.

Jilly had forgotten how beautiful Boone Ramsey's smile was. The fact was she hadn't seen it for years and years. But that didn't change the reality that, when he did smile, it seemed the sunshine was brighter somehow.

Still, she sighed with worry as she said, "And I'm sure he's already told everyone how you asked Grandpa for my hand and I went runnin' straight to him, askin' him to . . ." She stopped short—midsentence. Her cheeks blushed crimson with embarrassment, for she'd just revealed to Boone that she'd gone to Jack after hearing of Boone's proposal.

But Boone Ramsey—ever the hero—did not press her to finish what she was going to say. Simply he said, "Well, I'm hopin' that Reverend Dryer seein' us together, and that you weren't chained up and bein' whipped into marryin' me, will balance out any gossip ol' Jack the Jackass Taylor may have started up. After all, who are people gonna believe? The man of God in town or the ignoramus with a firm reputation as a tomcat, hmmm?"

Jilly nodded, hopeful that Boone was right in his estimations of whom folks would believe.

"It helps to have the reverend as a witness too . . . bein' that we don't want folks thinkin' I *had* to marry you and such," he added.

Jilly frowned, puzzled. "Well, why would folks think you *had* to marry me? You're the one who asked my grandpa for me in the first place. Wouldn't folks be more likely to think I *had* to marry you?"

Boone chuckled, as if he knew something she didn't. "Oh, it's no nevermind," he answered.

He looked at her—straight at her a moment—and Jilly was uncomfortable as he studied her.

"I'm right proud of you, Jilly Adams," he said then. "I thought you'd be sobbin' your eyes out by now. But you made it through the weddin' with the Reverend Dryer and leavin' your granny and everything, and you're still holdin' onto your tears. You're a strong young woman . . . a real strong young woman."

"Oh, I'm not so strong," she sighed. "In truth, I think I'm just sort of, you know, astonished or shocked or somethin'." She inhaled a breath of courage and then, before she could exhale her bravery away, asked, "Why did you ask my grandpa if you could marry me, Boone Ramsey? I know it has nothin' to do with fondness or anything. Why, you haven't spoken to me more than three or four times this summer. So why *did* you ask Grandpa for my hand?"

And there it was—the question Boone had been dreading since the moment Doolin Adams agreed to let him marry Jilly. Over the past two days, Boone had spent hours contemplating just how he should respond when Jilly asked him the question he wasn't ready to answer. He sure didn't want to fib to her, but he also knew that, just as he wasn't ready to tell her everything, she wasn't ready to hear it.

So he answered short and simple—truthfully too—without revealing the whole truth.

"I wanted a wife," he answered.

"You wanted a wife," Jilly repeated, her pretty eyebrows arching with suspicion. "That's it? You wanted a wife?"

Boone nodded but didn't offer anything more.

"Well, if you simply wanted a wife, then why me?" she asked next. "Why not one of the Havasham girls . . . or Ethel Farley, for that matter? Why me? And why so all of a sudden?"

Boone shrugged. "I wanted a wife . . . and I didn't want to wait any longer."

Jilly grinned at him. "But you still haven't told me why you chose me."

"I have my reasons," he answered, trying to skirt the details.

Jilly sighed with frustration. "Okay, I'm feelin' that you don't want to be very forthcomin' right now, and I'll respect that . . . for the time bein'. But do you suppose you could find it in your heart to tell me just one of those secret reasons you have? Please?"

Boone did have the heart, and he would share one reason with her—and it was a true and heartfelt reason.

"Because of the orange," he said.

Again she frowned, and he chuckled, for he'd figured she would've forgotten the incident long ago, and it seemed she had.

"The orange?" she asked. "You . . . you don't mean the orange I gave you that one Christmas when I was eight, do you?"

Boone smiled, pleased beyond words that she indeed did remember that orange.

"That is the very one I mean," he confessed.

At the perplexed and disbelieving expression on Jilly's face, Boone smiled—for he'd managed to distract her from pressing him further for more reasons as to why he'd chosen to ask Doolin Adams for his granddaughter's hand.

Jilly shook her head with skepticism. Was he serious? Did Boone just tell her that one of the reasons he chose to marry her was because of the silly little orange she'd given him years and years before?

Oh, the memory was still as fresh in Jilly's mind as if it had happened only a day before, even though it had been over ten years, in truth. But she couldn't believe Boone Ramsey still remembered it—thought kindly of her for it after all these years.

It was the Christmas the year Mr. and Mrs. Ramsey had died of the influenza, leaving their home and properties to their only son, Boone.

Boone Ramsey had astonished everyone when, at the tender age of fourteen, he'd managed to run the farm and ranch, to harvest his father's crops and everything else required to keep the properties productive, all by himself. Of course, he hadn't physically done all the work himself; he'd been wise enough and well trained enough by his father to keep on the hired hands and cowboys. Thus, the Ramsey properties were saved—even productive financially.

Still, for all the obvious successes the people of Mourning Dove Creek saw when young Boone Ramsey stepped into his father's boots, Jilly felt differently toward Boone. In truth, she'd always, always been sweet on Boone, thinking him the handsomest boy in town. But it wasn't just his good looks that touched Jilly that year but also the fact that she felt akin to him in having been orphaned at such a young age. She'd been even younger when she'd lost her parents. But then she'd had a loving home to go to—a grandma and grandpa that loved her and raised her as their own. Boone Ramsey had nothing—nothing but his properties and his work.

And so on Christmas morning of that year when Jilly awoke to find that St. Nicholas had indeed left gifts beneath the Christmas tree for her—and her stocking full of nuts and hard candies and the miracle of an orange—her thoughts leapt to poor lonesome Boone Ramsey. Jilly knew that oftentimes St. Nicholas didn't visit older children, and she was sure that, since Boone was now considered a young man, there had been no miracle of an orange left in one of his stockings.

Therefore, once her grandma and grandpa had fallen asleep in their parlor chairs, Jilly had tugged on her boots and coat, wrapped her warmest scarf about her neck and head, pulled on her mittens, and, with the miracle of an orange in her coat pocket, walked all the way to Boone Ramsey's house.

In those days, the Ramsey house was nearer to town. Boone had since built a new house some ways further out. But on that cold, crisp winter's morning, it wasn't such a long walk for a little girl with a purpose.

Jilly remembered that day so clearly—the bright, bright sunshine and cloudless sky. The Christmas Eve snow and frost that had fallen the night before sparkled clean and white beneath the canvas of light blue overhead. All the scents of Christmas were in the air as well—the comforting aroma of cedar fires, of turkeys and hams baking in ovens. Icicles hung from pine branches, tinkling like tiny crystal bells and adding the only sound to accompany the crunch, crunch, crunch of Jilly's own footsteps as she made her way to the Ramsey house.

Boone had answered her knock on the door, and Jilly smiled in that moment, remembering his tousled hair, his wary eyes, and the worn long underwear he'd been wearing when he opened it.

"Merry Christmas, Boone Ramsey," Jilly had greeted with a smile.

"Merry Christmas, Jilly," he said, his eyes brightening and a handsome smile spreading across his face.

"I've brought you this for Christmas," she told him. Taking the orange from her pocket, she held it in the cup of her tiny hands and offered it to him.

Even now, in her reverie, she could see the bright orange sitting in her little brown mittens, looking just as if she'd captured the sun somehow.

"Well, thank you, Jilly," Boone said, studying the orange with widened eyes full of wanting. "But I'm sure this is your Christmas orange. I wouldn't want to deprive you of it."

Jilly smiled. "St. Nicholas left it in my stockin'," she explained. "He left it for you, Boone." Then reaching out to take one of his hands, Jilly deposited the rare and precious piece of sweet citrus into Boone's warm hand. Smiling at him again, she said, "Merry Christmas, Boone Ramsey. Good-bye," and turned to start home.

"Thank you, Jilly Adams," Boone had called after her. "But don't you want me to drive you on home?"

"No, thank you," Jilly called over her shoulder.

"I like the sound the snow makes when I walk."

It had been that simple—that uncomplicated—just a gift of an orange to a boy Jilly thought might be lonely on Christmas.

Speaking her thoughts aloud, Jilly said, "But it was just an orange."

Boone looked at her, however, the brightness of his eyes somehow dimmed with a long-ago but unforgotten pain of loss.

"It was much more than an orange, Jill," he said. Then turning his attention back to the team, he added, "At least to me."

Goosebumps raced over Jilly's arms at Boone's shortening her name to just Jill. Somehow the intonation of his voice—the more grown-up sounding version of her name—affected her not just emotionally but physically. She liked that he'd shortened her name for her—liked that no one else ever had.

CHAPTER SIX

As Boone drove the team toward what would now be Jilly's home, she was surprised at the feeling of calm that began to develop inside her the closer they got to their destination. Gradually, the powerful sensations of trepidation, worry, and doubt started to subside. In their place, Jilly experienced an unexpected excitement.

She was married, and the fact of it was nearly unimaginable. But the fact that she was married to Boone Ramsey was even more inconceivable! Boone Ramsey—the handsomest man in town—Mourning Dove Creek's unspoken hero—the man she'd secretly harbored a powerful infatuation with for as long as she could remember knowing him. Silently allowing herself to admit that Boone had always intrigued her, attracted her, Jilly steadily began to confess to herself that Jack Taylor had been an error of judgment on her part—that having married Jack would have been a monumental mistake. Maybe she'd married a man she knew little about in Boone Ramsey—and married him for all the wrong reasons, including spite because of Jack's rejection. But in those moments, Jilly knew that marrying Boone Ramsey was a far better choice for any woman than ending up with a tomcat like Jack Taylor.

And so Jilly found that her heart was softening toward her situation—beginning to accept it—and, furthermore, look forward to it. Her grandpa had been right. Boone Ramsey was the best man in Mourning Dove Creek, so why shouldn't Jilly be glad, not to mention very flattered, that Boone had chosen her to marry? Even if his reason was the simple fact that he merely wanted a wife?

Jilly's nerves settled all the more when Boone pulled the team to a halt before his house—their house. Jilly grinned as she studied it, a slight feeling of lightheartedness catching in her bosom.

The house was obviously well built, with a sturdy front porch and plenty of windows to allow lots of sunshine inside. It was fresh and radiant in what looked to be a newer coat of whitewash and shutters that had been painted a dark red. Oh, it needed a woman's touch, perhaps—some curtains at the windows, some flowerpots on the porch—but the house that Boone Ramsey had built looked as if he'd built it with a wife in mind. In truth, Jilly was surprised by the welcoming nature of the home. Somehow she'd expected a shabby log cabin. After all, Boone had lived alone for more than ten years. It seemed he would've gotten comfortable with bachelorhood and built something simple and entirely masculine instead.

"Well, here we are," Boone said as he climbed down from the wagon.

"It's lovely!" Jilly exclaimed.

"I'm glad you like it," he said. As she stood to climb down from the wagon seat, Jilly felt Boone's hands encircle her waist. A quiet gasp escaped her as he effortlessly lifted her down.

"Thank you," she said.

He nodded. "I'll bring your trunk in here in a minute, but I best show you the house first."

Jilly gasped more audibly this time when Boone swept her up in the cradle of his powerful arms and started toward the house.

"Over the threshold. Ain't that the way they do it?" he asked as he managed to work the front door latch and send it swinging open, even with Jilly still in his arms.

As Boone stepped into the house with Jilly, her smile broadened. It was perfect! Simply perfect! The house was bright and cheerful—perhaps a little lacking in homey details such as doilies, curtains, and a jar of fresh flowers on the table, but Jilly wouldn't have wanted it any other way. A great unforeseen sense of having arrived home washed over Jilly as Boone allowed her feet to settle on the floor, and she felt like an artist viewing a fresh canvas as her imagination began to race with things to be done.

"Well, here you are," Boone sighed. "I cleaned it up for you . . . didn't want you thinkin' I live like a pig." He glanced around a bit. "This here's the entry, and you've got the parlor to the right . . . though I don't linger in it much." He nodded, indicating she look ahead. "The kitchen is right there, and the hallway to the left here leads to the bedrooms. There's three." Glancing at her, he grinned a little and said, "Come on, I'll show 'em to you."

At the mention of bedrooms, Jilly's grandma's oration on "a little added insight to the details of the goin's-on where the birds and the bees are concerned" began running through Jilly's mind, and a measure of her anxieties began to return.

When Boone gestured to the first bedroom on the hallway's right, however, her anxieties unpredictably transformed to a strange sort of disenchantment as he said, "This is the largest bedroom, and you can have this one. There's plenty of room at the foot of the bed for your trunk, and it's got the biggest wardrobe and chest of drawers. I'll use the room across the hallway here. I don't need much . . . just a place to drop after a long day."

"W-we have separate beds?" Jilly asked. "I-I mean, separate rooms?"

Boone's handsome brows puckered into a bewildered frown. "Well . . . I figured that's the way you'd want it. I'm not a fool, Jill. I know you married me because your grandpa worked it out . . . not because you wanted to." His frown softened, but he didn't smile. "I'm not gonna haul you to my bed and have my way with you tonight, if that's what you're worried about."

"You're not?" Jilly asked, so thoroughly relieved that she smiled.

Boone chuckled, "Well, you don't have to sound as thankful as all that. I'm not that ugly, am I?"

Jilly felt foolish and could think of nothing to say to reassure him that he wasn't ugly—that she was just innocent and frightened. So she just shook her head.

"Now the back room," Boone continued, striding toward the back of the house, "I kinda just put things in here that I don't know what else to do with. So you can just leave this mess alone. But the rest of the house . . . you do whatever you want with it, all right?"

Jilly frowned. "What do you mean? What would I do with it?"

Again Boone chuckled. "I don't know . . . women stuff. Tablecloths and doilies or whatever strikes your fancy to make it feel like your own home. I just need a place to hang my hat and lay me down to sleep."

"All right," Jilly said, suddenly feeling the emotion of happy anticipation come over her once more. "And . . . what about cookin'? I know you have hired hands out here somewhere. Do I cook for them too . . . or just you?"

"Just me," Boone answered. "I mean, if you don't mind—just me . . . and yourself, of course. The hands take care of themselves. You probably won't even see them much except here and there. Nope, just you and me. That's the only folks you'll be cookin' for."

Jilly sighed with relief. She'd been worried about having to cook for hired hands as well as a husband. She'd heard from other farmers' wives that it was twenty times the work, at least.

After looking into the back bedroom to see that it was indeed filled with piles of trunks, harnesses, old quilts, and other miscellany, Jilly turned to see Boone studying her. She blushed under the intensity of his enthralling gaze.

"I gotta admit . . . I thought you'd be bawlin' like a lost calf by now," he said, "bein' that you just married up with a complete stranger."

Jilly shrugged. "Oh, you're not a complete stranger," she told him. "After all, we shared an orange once, now didn't we?"

Boone was confused—entirely stupefied. He had expected Jilly Adams to be distraught, brought to the very depths of despair at having to marry him. Yet she hadn't cried a tear—not one. He wondered how it was possible that she hadn't expressed any of her fear and anxiety through tears. Then again, maybe she'd cried her eyes dry that first day—the day her grandpa told her Boone had asked for her hand.

Then again, he knew spite could carry a person a long way, and he knew she'd married him out of spite. He wasn't an idiot, after all. When he'd made the decision to ask for Jilly's hand, Boone had reconciled himself in understanding that she wouldn't adore him. Doolin Adams had assured Boone that Jilly would love him—if not instantly, then in the years to come. Oh, he didn't believe it, of course, so he had indeed reconciled himself to expecting nothing from Jilly—though he hoped for a pleasant camaraderie.

What he had expected though was a distraught young woman, sobbing over the hardship that had been thrust upon her. He knew the reality of it all would wash over Jilly at some point—probably that night when she was alone with a strange man in a strange house.

Shrugging a bit, Boone figured he'd just enjoy the fact that Jilly seemed to be putting off her despair for the time being.

"I'll go bring that trunk in for you now . . . so you can settle in a bit," Boone said. "Meanwhile, you just have a look around and figure out the kitchen or whatever you feel like doin'."

"I should help you with that trunk though," Jilly offered. "It's heavy."

"I'm sure I can handle it," Boone said, grinning at her. "You just wander a bit. I've got a few chores that need doin', and then I can take you out to the barn if you like . . . or to see the cattle or to choose your horse."

"Choose my horse?" Jilly asked.

"Well, yeah. I reckon you're gonna need one . . . unless you plan on hitchin' up the wagon every time you want to run into town and see your folks," Boone answered.

"No . . . no . . . the use of a horse would be wonderful," Jilly admitted, smiling.

"Then we'll take care of that business first off," Boone said. "Just let me finish up a few things, and then we'll see what we can find for you, all right?"

"All right," Jilly answered, trying not to smile too widely. But it was hard for Jilly not to feel absolutely giddy about having her own horse! She'd always dreamt of having her own horse—a horse she could saddle up and ride whenever the need or want to do so presented itself.

Thus, once Boone had carried in Jilly's trunk and deposited it at the foot of her bed, she kept busy with familiarizing herself with the kitchen and the rest of the house while Boone did some chores. But when at last he did return, walking with her out to the big barn of horse stables he owned—when he suggested a handsome buck-skin gelding and had Jilly feed the horse an apple—when the buckskin, Romeo, nuzzled her neck a bit with his velvety nose—Jilly was fairly certain she was the happiest girl in Mourning Dove Creek.

Yet as the sun began to set, Jilly discovered that all her newfound courage and excitement began to evaporate as quickly as it had appeared.

She'd made a delicious supper of ham and biscuits with butter—both of which were so much more delicious when paired with the sweet, fresh honey Boone had collected from a beehive he'd found holed up in an old maple tree. Boone had relished the supper Jilly had prepared, complimenting her over and over on how wonderful it had been.

Yet the lower the sun sank in the west and the darker it grew, the greater Jilly's returning anxieties became.

What had she done? She'd married a near stranger! Worse, she'd done so out of spite—spite directed at Jack Taylor—and even a little spite directed at her grandpa and grandma. How could they do this to her? Send her off to live with some man she hardly knew?

Jilly tried to mask her fears and insecurities, tried to appear perfectly calm and settled as she shared supper with Boone, as they sat in the parlor afterward sharing light conversation.

She knew that Boone was not an idiot, however. Jilly had no doubt that Boone could read her countenance as bedtime drew nearer.

And he proved it when he rose, at last, and said, "Well, I'm plum tuckered out. And I'm sure you are too, Jill. So why don't we head off to bed? Separate beds, of course."

"It h-has been a long day, it seems," she managed to stammer as he rose from his chair and slipped his suspenders off his shoulders.

"And tomorrow will be the same," Boone said.

Jilly's eyes widened as, standing right there in the parlor, Boone Ramsey stripped off his shirt—right there—right in front of her! She tried not to stare at him as he stood bare-chested directly in front of her. But the fact was she couldn't help herself! Boone Ramsey's broad shoulders and chest were discernable enough when he was dressed, but when he was undressed, the full revelation of his muscular, bronzed torso was astonishing!

As Boone started to toss the shirt over the back of his chair, he paused, saying, "Oh. I suppose I better quit leavin' my clothes layin' all over the house now, huh?" Yet as he stood glancing around the room, as if he weren't sure what to do with the shirt, Jilly felt a grin of amusement tug the corner of her lips.

"There's a basket I put on the back porch," she told him. "Just toss it in the basket. That's where we'll put things that need washin' . . . if that's all right with you."

Boone's handsome brows arched in admiration of a good idea. "Hmmm. I never woulda thought of doin' that. I just sort of left everything layin' here and there . . . then gathered it up when it needed washin'. A basket on the back porch, huh?" He shook his head and smiled. "Sometimes I think I'm dumber than an ox."

Jilly smiled, thinking that it was somehow endearing that Boone had never thought to put his soiled clothes all in one place.

But her smile faded the instant he turned to leave. "What on earth?" she exclaimed, leaping to her feet. "What happened?"

Boone turned back to face her, a puzzled frown on his face. "Where?" he asked, glancing around the room.

"There!" Jilly exclaimed, pointing to him. "At your back!"

Boone sighed. "Oh, that. Just a cut. An ax fell off the barn wall and hit me there. I had Doc Havasham stitch it up the other day, since I couldn't reach it myself. But then that whole mess with the Lillingston boy ripped it open again, and the doc had to do some more stitchin'. It's fine now though."

"Fine?" Jilly asked in lingering consternation. "It's dreadful! It must be excruciatin'! It's not even bandaged!"

But Boone simply shrugged. "It just needs to dry out a bit more . . . scab over some. It doesn't hurt near as much now as it did," he said, working his arm on the same side of his body.

Yet as Jilly lay in her new bed late that night, weeping and sniffling for missing her old bed—the soft, comfortable, familiar bed she'd slept in for the past fourteen years—she couldn't keep the image of Boone's terrible wound from hovering at the forefront of her mind. In all her life, she'd never had a wound as severe as the one Boone seemed to shrug off like it were only a cat scratch. It made her wonder what other injuries or wounds he might endure in the future; it made her fearful of his well-being.

And mingled with Jilly's worry over Boone's well-being was the angst she was beginning to feel with herself over Jack Taylor, over what she was realizing were her true feelings where Jack was concerned—and those feelings weren't love as she'd thought they'd been. And as she lay in her new, albeit large and very comfortable bed, worrying over Boone's injury, astonished at how even more attractive he'd appeared while standing in the parlor shirtless before her—as she lay there missing her grandma and grandpa, her childhood, her parents, and everything else she could possible miss—she wept—wept and sniffled. Yet it wasn't the weeping of heartbreak but that of melancholy, of knowing nothing would ever be the same—not ever again. As she lay in bed, the evening breeze and moonlight wafting through the open window—even as the thought passed through her mind that she should see about making some curtains for her bedroom window—Jilly wept in knowing that her life would never be the same. And though she knew that life as Boone Ramsey's wife would be secure and maybe even happy one day, Jilly knew that the blithe and easy days of childhood and adolescence were gone—never to be recaptured.

Boone sighed. There it was—what he'd expected all along—the soft weeping, the sniffling of a woman crying her heart out. As Boone lay in his bed gazing at the moonbeams softly streaming through his open window, he promised himself that one day he'd beat the wadding out of Jack the Jackass Taylor. The man deserved nothing less for what he'd done to Jilly Adams's heart, not to mention Dina Havasham's.

Boone was just thankful he'd overheard the conversation between Doolin Adams and Doc Havasham—for who knew what that tomcat, Jack Taylor, might have done to destroy Jilly if she'd been trapped in his claws any longer? Oh, he knew Jilly was miserable now, but at least she'd be cared for, provided for, and protected under his roof. And Doolin Adams knew it too—and that gave Boone a great measure of comfort.

Yep, Boone had been lucky. He'd snatched Jilly from the jaws of misery, just as he'd always promised himself he would do. From the day the sweet little girl had walked all the way from town out to his empty, lonely farmhouse one Christmas morning ten years before—from the moment she'd showered him with compassion with that sweet, succulent, beautiful orange—well, Boone Ramsey had promised himself then and there that he would always watch over Jilly Adams. As he'd stood at the threshold of his lonesome farmhouse that first Christmas after losing his parents—as he'd watched little Jilly Adams happily skipping away through the sparkling, frost-sifted snow—Boone Adams had vowed to keep her from harm, no matter what he would have to do to do it. And even though he could hear her quiet weeping and knew that she was unhappy in being forced to marry him, Boone knew he'd kept the vow he'd made so long ago; he'd kept her from harm. He'd married her out from under Jack Taylor, snatching her away from further heartache and misery. Oh, she didn't realize it, of course—and maybe she never would. But Boone would do everything he could to make sure that Jilly Adams was cared for. And he could only hope that, in the end, she would find a measure of happiness in her life with him.

As Boone closed his eyes and exhaled a heavy sigh of fatigue and anxiety for Jilly's sake, a memory flittered across his mind: an image of a little girl and an orange. And for a moment he could remember the cool, sweet, delicious sensation of that long-ago orange as it juiced in his mouth before sliding down his throat. That orange—it was still the sweetest taste Boone Ramsey had ever known.

CHAPTER SEVEN

"He's a beautiful horse, Jilly!" Effie exclaimed, patting Romeo's nose.

"Yes, he is," Doolin agreed, studying the horse's flanks. "Boone Ramsey sure knows a good horse when he sees one. Has this boy got a good disposition?"

"Oh yes!" Jilly confirmed. "He's a sweetheart!" She nuzzled Romeo's nose, and he let go a quiet whinny of pleasure.

"And how was your first day as Mrs. Boone Ramsey?" Jilly's grandmother asked.

Jilly shrugged. "Fine, I guess," she answered.

"Fine?" her grandpa exclaimed with a grin of amusement. "Fine? Well, if that don't beat all. A woman's first day of marriage—first night away from home—and she says it was fine?"

Jilly shrugged again. "Well, I don't know how else to describe it. I mean, in truth, after the weddin' ceremony, I spent most of the day thinkin' on how shallow and stupid I was where Jack Taylor and all that nonsense was concerned."

"How excitin' for Boone," Doolin chuckled under his breath.

"Hush, Doolin!" Effie scolded, shoving a scolding elbow into her husband's ribs. "And what are you goin' on about, Jilly? What do you mean you spent most of the day thinkin' on how shallow and stupid you've been?"

Jilly shook her head. "Well, I did," she said. "I mean, I cooked a good enough supper for Boone—or at least I hope I did—and I got my personal things in order and such. But mostly, I just thought a lot about . . . well . . . thought about . . . wondered about why I ever fell into the association with Jack Taylor that I did. I mean, I'm more mad and humiliated than I am hurt by him for bein' such a tomcat and puttin' me off. I find that I don't miss him a lick. I'm not even sad that he didn't really care for me . . . just angry that I wasted my time. The more I think about it, the more I'm convinced that the only reason I liked Jack in the first place was because all the other girls in town fawn over him and told me I was crazy not to let him court me once he asked."

"So you spent the day in evaluatin' yourself, hmmm? Appraisin' your past, so to speak," Doolin sighed. "It's a good thing to do every now and again, Jilly. In fact, it's necessary."

"Yes, it is," Effie agreed. "Seems you figured a lot of things out after you married Boone Ramsey. And that's a good start to a marriage."

"I don't know that it's anything like a real

marriage," Jilly began. "All we did was chores, horses, and supper."

"Sounds like regular life to me," Doolin chuckled. His smile broadened then, and he winked at Jilly as he asked, "And how was the weddin' night, by the way?"

"Doolin Adams!" Effie exclaimed. "You know better than to ask such questions!" Yet in the next breath, Jilly's grandma turned to her and asked, "Well? How *did* it go?"

Jilly shrugged. "Fine, I guess. I slept well enough, especially for bein' in a new place . . . and even considerin' the big ol' bed in my room."

"*Your* room?" her grandma and grandpa exclaimed in unison.

"Yes," Jilly affirmed—though she found she felt cheated somehow, or as if she'd failed at something. "Boone has his room, and I have mine. He said he knew I married him because Grandpa worked it out and not because I wanted to. And so he wasn't gonna haul me to his bed and have his way with me . . . whatever that means."

Doolin frowned. "I always took Boone Ramsey for a gentleman but not an idiot."

"Doolin!" Effie scolded in a whisper. Putting her arm around Jilly's shoulders, Effie soothed, "All in good time, honey. You don't worry about not havin' a weddin' night yet. It will all come along in good time."

But Jilly shrugged and said, "I'm not worried about it." Though, in truth, she kind of was—especially because of the way her grandpa had reacted.

"Well, let me just say this, Jilly," Doolin began then. "You don't worry another minute about Jack Taylor and his shenanigans. Everything we go through in life—whether it's good or bad, embarrassin' or brings praise—everything teaches us somethin', and I 'spect you learned a lot from ol' Tomcat Jack. For one thing, you learnt the difference between infatuation and love . . . and that's an important little item to know in life."

Jilly nodded but glanced away in feeling the fool anyway. "I suppose everyone in town knows I went to Jack in a storm of tears and made a fool of myself."

Jilly looked up when neither her grandpa nor grandma responded right away. They were exchanging glances and smiles.

"What?" Jilly asked. "It's worse than I thought? The gossip, I mean?"

"Not at all," Doolin answered. "Seems Reverend Dryer was so impressed by the passion he saw sparkin' between you and Boone when Boone kissed you at your ceremony yesterday that he was all over town yesterday with tales of undeniable true love."

Effie smiled. "Yep. Half the town believes

Jack Taylor's story that Doolin made you marry Boone Ramsey . . . and the other half thinks you and Boone were secretly in love for months and months."

Jilly frowned. "But in the end of it, folks are more likely to believe Jack and the truth than the Reverend Dryer's misconception."

"Not at all," Doolin countered. "Fact is, folks know Jack Taylor is a tomcat . . . just as well as they know Reverend Dryer ain't about to lie."

Jilly shook her head, unconvinced. "And the worst part is . . . my stupid, silly foolishness will reflect on Boone. Everyone in Mournin' Dove will be wonderin' what *really* happened . . . why he *really* married me."

"Oh, don't give it so much of your thinkin' attention, Jilly honey," Effie soothed. "Even if people are wonderin' what the whole truth is, in a week or two they'll be onto nippin' at somethin' else that's gone on. You just worry about takin' care of yourself and your new husband . . . about settlin' in and makin' a good, comfortable home for the both of you."

"That's right, honey," Doolin agreed. "People are gonna talk no matter if they're chewin' on the truth or makin' up fairy stories. So you just live your life from here on, all right?"

Jilly nodded—though she still felt like the biggest ignoramus to walk the earth. What had she been thinking where Jack was concerned?

How had she let herself be so silly and foolish? Still, she figured she wasn't the first girl to mistake infatuation for something deeper. She'd have to move past it—quit thinking on it and stop beating herself. The truth was she couldn't undo it. All she could do was what her very wise grandpa had said—learn from it.

"Now let me get that cinnamon you needed for your supper tonight, honey," Effie began, "and then you can be on your way home. You wouldn't want Boone comin' home to find you still gone and think you run off, now would you?"

Jilly grinned. "No, I wouldn't," she giggled. "But he knows I was plannin' on comin' up to get the cinnamon, so I'm sure he wouldn't think such a thing."

"Well, you never know," Effie said as she turned and hurried into the house.

Jilly sighed with a sense of being overwhelmed suddenly. But when she looked up to her grandpa, it was to see him grinning at her—as if he knew something she didn't.

"What?" she asked, smiling at him.

"You like Boone, don't you?" he asked in return.

Jilly felt a bit of pink heat rise to her cheeks. "I've always liked him. You probably knew that better than I did."

"Yes, I did. But you like him more than you realized, don't you?" he pressed.

Jilly shrugged. "Maybe. And that's all I'm sayin'."

Doolin laughed. "Well, it's enough to tell me I was right."

But Jilly wagged an index finger at her grandpa and scolded, "Now don't be sittin' your high horse, Grandpa. Just because I admit that I've always found Boone Ramsey intriguin' doesn't mean that I was ready to marry him . . . or that everything will work out as sweet and perfect as Grandma's peach pie, you know."

"We'll see," her grandpa said. "We'll see."

As Jilly rode home—home to the pretty house where she was now wife to a man she hardly knew—her mind still lingered on her own foolishness regarding Jack Taylor. Glancing up to the blue, summer sky—to the billowy, white clouds sitting on the horizon, looking like freshly popped cotton bolls—she tried to distract her thoughts from Jack Taylor to the beauty of the day.

The wildflowers of so many varieties—orange and scarlet paintbrush, purple columbine, sunflowers—covered the earth like a pretty patchwork quilt. The aroma of summer still hung in the air—of sunshine and green grass, the wildflowers and rich soil. A breeze caught a strand of Jilly's hair, and a large yellow butterfly lit on Romeo's forehead for a moment.

But even for the glory of the day, Jilly could not keep from thinking of what a fool she had been. Over and over she told herself that Jack and her nonsense were in the past; there was nothing that could be done about it now. All she could do was live in the present and look to the future. Yet humiliation is a clinging vine—a clinging weed—and Jilly knew it would bind her for some time.

She was nearly home when she saw Boone riding toward her. Jilly felt a smile curve her lips as she watched him approach. Oh, could the man sit a saddle! He was handsome, no matter what he was doing—a man—not a boy like Jack.

Jilly reined in Romeo, though she'd been riding him at a slow walk anyway. Her smile broadened when Boone reined in his horse beside her, for he was smiling already as well.

"Hey, wanna have some fun?" he asked.

Though his question as a greeting was unexpected, Jilly answered, "Of course," with a delighted giggle.

Boone nodded, chuckled, and said, "Then follow me."

Turning his mount east, Jilly bit her lip with excitement as she followed. What could Boone be up to? She had no idea. But by the twinkle of mischief evident in his eyes, Jilly just knew it had to be tomfoolery of some sort, and she was wildly impatient to see what it was.

• • •

"We'll have to go real slow and not make a sound," Boone whispered as he lay next to Jilly in the tall grass near the pond.

Jilly nodded and gritted her teeth to keep from giggling. If she and Boone were discovered, the fun would be over—and the consequences could be uncomfortable, to say the least.

"Okay then . . . let's go," Boone whispered.

As Jilly began to crawl toward the fallen tree where the three adolescent boys had deposited their clothing before wading naked into the pond, she could feel the smile on her face as wide as the Mississippi. When Boone had ridden up to her on her way home from her grandma and grandpa's place, asking her if she wanted to have some fun, she had never imagined that he meant for them to steal the clothing of three boys he'd seen swimming in the nude.

Boone had explained that snatching the clothes of naked swimmers was the oldest prank in the world—and that Willy Lillingston, Arthur Farley, and Davey Graham were nearly asking to be pranked by taking such a risk as swimming in the nude. Naturally, Jilly was wildly intrigued. She'd never done anything so brazen and daring in all her life!

Boone had explained how he and Jilly were going to crawl on their stomachs through the tall grass toward the old fallen oak that lay on one side of the pond. The boys had left their clothes scattered on the old tree, and the tree was big enough to hide Boone and Jilly's approach—if they stayed low enough.

Of course, Jilly was certain the boys would get in all kinds of terrible trouble if they had to go skipping home without a stitch of clothing. But Boone assured her that they would put the boys' clothes somewhere that the boys could find them—just not too easily.

Thus Jilly had instantly agreed to help Boone prank the three boys—all three of whom were approximately thirteen years of age and all three of whom had about driven the entire town of Mourning Dove Creek to lunacy the Halloween almost a year before, with their own pranks of stealing fence posts and gates, tipping over outhouses, and other such rambunctious deeds.

Boone had been out checking a fence line when he'd heard laughter and seen the three boys swimming in the nude. He'd told Jilly that of course he could've snatched their clothes on his own, but he figured the prank would be so much more entertaining if he had her to share the fun with him. So he'd ridden out to find her—and now Jilly was crawling through the grass next to him.

Once they reached the fallen tree, however, Boone paused before reaching up to snatch any clothing.

He put an index finger to his lips and mouthed, *Hold on,* to Jilly. Then, slowly, he raised himself just enough so that he could see over the log.

"They're still in the water," he whispered. "We don't want them to see us take their clothes or it'll ruin everything. So just pull one thing at a time off . . . really slowly so there's no quick motion to catch their eye, all right?"

Jilly again gritted her teeth to keep from giggling with amusement. She nodded.

She watched as Boone reached up, slowly pulling a pair of trousers off the fallen tree. "Like that," he assured her.

Jilly reached up and did the same with a shirt, and Boone smiled with approval.

Carefully Boone and Jilly snatched three pairs of trousers, three shirts, and three pairs of boys' underwear. Wadding them up in their arms, they then turned on their bellies and hurriedly crawled away to the safety of the nearby tree line.

"Now then," Boone began, although quietly, "let's just toss everything here and there under the trees, all right?"

"Yes," Jilly giggled.

She watched as Boone tossed a pair of trousers onto a low tree limb—threw a pair of underwear up a little higher. He chuckled with amusement, and Jilly thought how delightful the sound of his laughter was.

"I wish we could see the expressions on their

faces when they realize their clothes have gone missin'," Jilly whispered, "though I have no desire to see a bunch of boys runnin' around naked."

"Well, the horses will be fine where we tied them up back there in the trees, and the boys won't want to waste any time lookin' to see who pranked them," Boone explained. "So we'll just climb up high in one of these trees close to where we're leavin' these clothes, and they'll never know we're witnessin' it all."

Jilly's smile broadened. "Perfect!" she giggled.

And true as his word, a few minutes later, Jilly was nestled snug as a bug on a large limb some ways up in the lofty canopy of a strong old maple tree. She was a good tree-climber herself, but Boone was a gentleman and had helped her to climb high enough so that they could see the boys but where the boys would have to look very hard to see them.

"And now we wait," Boone sighed—a handsome smile of triumph perfectly complementing the twinkle in his eyes.

Jilly smiled at him—sighed with experiencing a moment of pure contentment.

"This was a good idea you had," she whispered. "I'm glad you asked me along to help."

"Me too," Boone said in a lowered voice. "I thought you might enjoy somethin' a little out of the everyday." He paused a moment and then asked, "How was your visit with your folks? Have you forgiven your grandpa for makin' you marry me yet?"

"My visit was wonderful," she answered. Casting her gaze away from him a moment, she added, "And though I still don't understand it all . . . yes . . . I've forgiven him."

"And have you forgiven me?"

Jilly looked back to Boone to find him frowning with concern. She blushed as the realization washed over her that she'd never been angry with Boone for asking to marry her—not once.

"I have nothin' to forgive you for," she said. "After all, all you did was ask Grandpa. He's the one who agreed to it. I don't see where you did anything wrong." She was quiet a moment and then asked, "Why *did* you ask for me? There're plenty of girls in Mournin' Dove Creek that are at a marriageable age. If you simply wanted a wife the way you said you did . . . then why me? And don't say it was because of the orange at Christmas so long back."

"I have my reasons," Boone answered.

Jilly rolled her eyes with exasperation. "That doesn't tell me anything at all," she mumbled.

"I know," Boone agreed. Then suddenly he straightened on the limb where he sat and whispered, "Shhh. They're comin' out of the water right now."

Jilly looked to see that, indeed, Boone was

correct. Willy Lillingston, Arthur Farley, and Davey Graham were wading toward the grassy bank of the pond—toward the old fallen tree.

"Oh my, no!" Jilly exclaimed in a whisper as she quickly covered her eyes with both hands. "They'll be naked as the day they were born!"

She heard Boone chuckle, "Yes, they will."

Jilly felt Boone's hand on her knee then and spread several of her fingers to peer at him.

He was grinning at her with amused reassurance. "They're just boys, Jill. Do you really want to miss the fun just for worryin' about bein' so proper? They're hardly out of their diapers."

It was true. She didn't want to miss the fun—the horrified expressions, the panic she was sure would follow when the boys found their clothes had disappeared.

"Okay then. I'll just watch through my fingers," Jilly answered.

Boone seemed satisfied with her choice—though he did continue to smile with amusement.

Through the spaces between her fingers, Jilly watched as the boys talked and laughed without a care in the world as they stepped out of Mourning Dove Pond and into the grass at the bank. She watched as they shoved one another in teasing, sauntering toward the fallen tree entirely unsuspecting.

However, Jilly's hands moved from her eyes,

where they'd been impairing her clear vision of the nude boys, to cover her mouth in order to dampen the volume of the laughter that filled her mouth when the boys arrived at the fallen tree to find nothing but their socks and boots.

The scene that played out before Jilly and Boone was absolutely the most hysterical thing Jilly had ever witnessed in all her life! When Willy Lillingston, Arthur Farley, and Davey Graham arrived at the fallen tree to see that their clothes were missing, all three boys began hollering like their hair was on fire! Instantly their hands went to their fronts below their waist in sad attempts to cover their private parts as they looked around for any sign of their clothing.

From his place on the large tree limb next to Jilly, Boone was trying to stay as quiet as possible, yet laughing so hard that tears of mirth were gathering at the outer corners of his eyes. Jilly held her hands clamped as hard as possible over her mouth to muffle her own laughter—though she figured, with the way the three naked boys were carrying on, they wouldn't have heard a tornado setting down next to them.

Scrambling this way and that, Willy, Arthur, and Davey began searching for their missing attire.

"I found my drawers!" Davey Graham shouted at last. "I think our clothes are over this way, boys!"

Wiping the moisture produced by profound amusement from his eyes, Boone looked to Jilly, putting an index finger to his lips. "Shhh. Here they come," he whispered.

"Who the devil done this?" Willy Lillingston grumbled as he fished his trousers down off a tree limb. "I swear, if I ever find out who done this . . . I'll hang 'em high!"

"You fellers don't think it was girls who done this, do you?" Arthur asked.

Jilly bit her lip as all three boys then blushed and began looking around again. Hands over their privates once more, they quickly gathered their clothes.

"This ain't funny!" Willy yelled to the wind. "Whoever you are . . . if you think this is funny . . . well, it ain't!"

Jilly watched Boone as he watched the boys angrily pulling on their clothes. His smile was so bright and so big it was dazzling! His eyes were shining with pure merriment.

Oh, but he was handsome! He always had been. But something about seeing Boone so relaxed and entertained—something about the way he'd included Jilly in his plans to prank the boys—it made Boone Ramsey appear even more attractive in those moments.

"And there they go," Boone chuckled, drawing Jilly's attention back to the boys.

As she watched the humiliated and infuriated

boys trudging off back toward town, Jilly asked, "Do you think they'll tell on us?"

Boone looked at her, smiling and frowning simultaneously. "Hell no!" he exclaimed, still relishing the foregoing entertainment. "They won't tell a soul."

"But how do you know?" Jilly asked. "What if they tell their folks and then their folks figure out it was us?"

But Boone just sighed with triumph and chuckled. "Honey, there ain't no way anybody would ever figure out it was us . . . even if one of them did tell someone. But I can promise you that they're not gonna tell a soul—least for another ten or fifteen years." He shrugged, adding, "And besides, it happens to everyone sooner or later."

"What happens to everyone?" Jilly asked. "Gettin' your clothes stolen while you're swimmin'?"

Boone nodded. "Gettin' your clothes stolen while you're swimmin' naked," he answered.

Jilly's eyes widened. "Did it happen to you?"

"Hell yes!" Boone chuckled. "When I was about the same age. Me and a couple other boys skipped school to come on down to the pond and go swimmin' in the nude. When we were finished—'cause we started thinkin' we best be gettin' home before our folks found out we'd skipped school and started wonderin' where we were—we came up out of this very same pond to find our clothes missin'. The only difference was we never found 'em."

"What? You never found your clothes?" Jilly gasped.

Boone shook his head. "Nope. I had to walk on home naked as a jaybird," he answered. "I can't tell you how glad I was that our home was so far out from town. I was lucky too . . .'cause Mama was out feedin' the chickens, and my daddy was harvestin'."

"But what about the other boys? The ones you were with?" Jilly asked.

"Truth be told, they were fortunate, in the end of it. Mrs. Brooks had been doin' laundry that day. She had her boys' clothes hangin' out on the line, so Clarence and Robert just stole some of the Brooks' boys' clothes and headed on home."

"Clarence Farley? He was swimmin' with you that day?" Jilly giggled.

"Yep," Boone confirmed. "But Robert's family moved away shortly after that. Not sure you remember the Spaffords."

Jilly shook her head and said, "Nope. I don't."

Boone shrugged. "Anyway . . . all boys get caught sooner or later. If you're gonna swim naked, you're gonna get caught."

"So that's why you quit, hmm?" Jilly asked, smiling. "Because you finally got caught?"

Boone smiled. "I never said I quit," he answered. "I've just never been caught again."

Jilly blushed, asking, "B-but you quit when you grew up, right?"

"Nope," Boone answered. "In fact, that day I rode out here to find that little Lillingston boy washin' away down the crick . . . I was actually out this way, plannin' on havin' myself a nice, refreshin' swim."

Jilly's eyes widened, her blush deepening. "Really?"

Boone smiled. "Yep."

He began to climb down from the tree then. "You just follow me down, Jill," he instructed. "I'll go slow and help you if you need me to."

Jilly did climb down and slowly. But not because she lacked sure footing or was afraid she'd take a tumble—more for the fact her mind was reeling with the sudden awareness she now owned of men and boys and their rascally habits of swimming naked.

CHAPTER EIGHT

The days following the pranking of the three naked, swimming boys were less eventful by comparison perhaps, but very interesting all the same. As Jilly hung freshly washed sheets on the clothesline at the back of the house, several of the conversations she'd shared with Boone at their supper table lingered in her mind. During the past few evenings, she and Boone had talked lightheartedly about individual memories of their childhoods, discussed concerns over some of their fellow citizens of Mourning Dove Creek, and laughed together over trivial tidbits of life and living. They'd shared opinions on politics, guessed at what kind of weather the coming months would bring, and shared different family traditions they'd experienced.

And as Jilly thought about it all, she had the sudden realization that not only were her conversations with Jack Taylor pitifully shallow but also that she and Boone thought quite alike in every regard, sharing similar views and opinions on every subject. Jilly also realized how well suited their characters were in humor. Nearly every conversation they had eventually led them to laughter.

Again Jilly was struck by her own stupidity in the past—the very recent past—Jack Taylor the tomcat, nothing but a boy, whether or not his physical maturity tried to prove differently. Not one conversation she'd ever shared with Jack had been as stimulating as every sentence she exchanged with Boone.

Pulling another wet sheet from the basket at her feet, Jilly whipped it to shake it out—whipped it several times unnecessarily in order to vent her ever-lingering frustration with herself where Jack Taylor was concerned. Oh, she'd been an idiot! And yet the past was past, and there was nothing she could change about it. Thus, she exhaled a heavy sigh and pinned the poor whipped sheet to the line.

As she did so, however, the sun glinted on the gold band on her left ring finger. Jilly smiled as she studied the ring closely a moment. Just the night before, as she and Boone had been discussing his parents, Boone had casually mentioned that the wedding bands he'd brought to their wedding had belonged to his own mother and father. In fact, on her deathbed, Boone's mother had requested that he remove her ring, and that of his dying father, and keep them safe until he married one day.

Jilly found that, since the moment Boone

had told her the story, she had an even greater appreciation for the ring he'd placed on her finger on their wedding day—for it had belonged to his mother once, and Jilly liked to imagine that his mother was in heaven, smiling down with approval at Jilly's efforts to be a good wife to her son.

Picking up the empty basket at her feet, Jilly started back into the house. Yet as she stepped up onto the back porch, she saw that Boone had discarded one of his shirts over the porch railing. The sight of Boone's abandoned shirt caused a giggle to tickle Jilly's throat—for, try as he might, Boone hadn't quite discarded his old habit of disrobing whenever he had a mind to and leaving certain articles of clothing hither and yon as he did so. Gathering the shirt into one hand, Jilly drew it to her face, inhaling the scent of new grass, wood smoke, and fried ham—scents she'd quickly come to associate with her husband.

Tossing the shirt into the basket in her arms, she smiled as she thought of Boone just the night before, sliding his suspenders from his shoulders to hang from his waist as he stripped off his shirt in readying for bed. Jilly felt her smile broaden and a warm blush pink up her cheeks as she thought of how wildly attractive Boone was in such a state of undress. Oh, she knew she could never confess the fact she adored the time Boone spent roaming the house in just his trousers, hanging suspenders, and socks each evening for an hour or so before he retired. But she was glad he owned the habit, for he was fiercely alluring in such a state.

Jilly found then that her reminiscing of Boone's appearance in the evenings before bed drew her thoughts to wondering, as she often did throughout the day, if an occasion would ever arise where she might be kissed by him again. In truth, the kiss he'd kissed her with at their wedding ceremony had been incredible! Though it had taken her several days to admit it to herself, Jilly had quickly found that the moment of the kiss was the clearest in her mind of the entire day they were married. She'd thought it was astonishment at first—the mingled weakness and elation that had come over her when Boone had kissed her. But she knew it was far more—even then—and she wanted Boone to kiss her again.

Still, what were the chances he ever would? Slim to none, she figured. He hadn't even taken advantage of his "husbandly rights" (as she'd once heard it called) on their wedding night. So why ever would he want to kiss her again?

Jilly's heart leapt with delight as she heard the rhythm of horse hooves and turned to see Boone riding up to the barn. She watched as he quickly dismounted and hurried into the barn, returning with a large coil of rope. He was frowning, and Jilly's initial delight at seeing him turned to anxiety. Setting the basket on the porch, she hurried across the grassy space between the house and barn.

"Is somethin' wrong?" she asked—though she already sensed something was.

Boone nodded. "Yep. The little Graham girl fell into an old well out on the Graham place. Graham doesn't have a long enough length of rope to send someone in after her, and our place is closest."

Jilly frowned. "You're plannin' on climbin' down after her, aren't you?"

Boone shrugged as he attached the coil of rope to his saddle. "Someone has to go in after her. She'll drown here pretty quick if I don't."

"Why can't her daddy go in after her . . . or her brother?" Jilly asked as a strange, unfamiliar sort of anger began to grow inside her.

Boone puffed a breath of disgust. "Her daddy? Wallace Graham is too . . . too big around to fit down the well. And I wouldn't send Davey in after her and risk havin' two children trapped."

"But . . . but what if you're hurt or—" Jilly began.

"I'll be fine," Boone interrupted. He mounted his horse and smiled down at her. "And I'll be back in time for lunch."

Then he rode off at a gallop in the direction from whence he'd come.

Jilly frowned. It wasn't that she didn't care for

the little Graham girl's well-being—she did! It was just that, in that moment, she was worried for Boone's. Why did it always have to be Boone Ramsey that saved everybody's life?

Jilly knew that her frustration wouldn't be eased—not as long as Boone was gone. Marching to the barn, she saddled Romeo and rode off on her own undertaking then—a visit with her grandpa and grandma in an attempt to settle her suddenly very rattled nerves.

"It's who he is, Jilly honey," Doolin Adams said. "It's always been Boone Ramsey folks go runnin' to when they're in trouble, and it ain't likely to change."

"But what if Boone ends up gettin' hurt down in that well?" Jilly asked. "What if one day, while he's savin' somebody else, he gets injured . . . or worse?"

"Then that's somethin' we'll all have to handle if and when it happens," Doolin answered.

"But you can't sit around always expectin' the worst, honey," Effie added. "The good Lord watches over men like Boone Ramsey. They put themselves in danger helpin' others . . . so the Lord takes extra good care of them. You have to have faith in that."

"I know," Jilly mumbled.

She sighed, attempting to have the faith to know that Boone would be cared for by a greater power while he was helping the Grahams' little girl. She closed her eyes a moment—listened to the rhythm of her grandma's rocker—breathed deeply the soothing scent of her grandpa's pipe smoke. Yet it was strange to her—the sense that, even though everything around her was familiar and most beloved, she didn't feel like she was home. She kept thinking of the house she and Boone shared, of what she was going to cook for supper, and how handsome Boone would look sitting across the table from her as they shared their evening meal.

"Well, I probably shouldn't linger," Jilly said, opening her eyes. "I need to run into the general store and buy a bit more sugar and then make sure somethin's ready for lunch when Boone gets back."

She heard her grandpa chuckle and looked up to see Doolin and Effie Adams exchange knowing glances.

"What?" she asked.

"Nothin'," Doolin answered. "We're just glad to see you're settlin' in so quick."

Jilly couldn't help but smile and say, "Oh, you two think you're so clever . . . marryin' me off to Boone Ramsey the way you did. You're so sure I'm gonna be eatin' crow and thankin' you for doin' it one day."

"Yep," Doolin chuckled.

Her grandma smiled and winked at her, and

Jilly giggled as she stood and placed an affectionate kiss on each of their foreheads.

"Don't go gettin' too full of yourselves now," she said. "You're only at the beginnin' of this book, you know."

"We know," Effie said. "Now you run on and get what you need from the general store before your husband gets home with his stomach growlin' like an old grizzly."

"I will," Jilly said. "I love you both. Bye-bye."

"Bye, honey," Effie called as Jilly left the parlor and headed for the front door.

"Bring me some of those brown sugar cookies you make next time you're by," Doolin added.

"All right, Grandpa. I will," Jilly called in return. She smiled and shook her head with amusement. Her grandpa was a slave to anything sweet. She'd be sure to bring him something sweet very soon.

Taking hold of Romeo's reins, Jilly decided to lead him to the general store instead of riding. After all, it wasn't a long distance, and she felt like walking.

"Hey there, Miss Jilly," Arthur Farley greeted with a smile as he passed her in the street. "Sure is a pretty day, ain't it?"

"It sure is," Jilly agreed. And then—then a mischief she'd only felt once before in all her life began to bubble up inside her, and she added, "It's so warm and dry. Kind of puts a body in mind of maybe takin' a swim down in Mournin' Dove Pond, doesn't it?"

As Arthur's smile faded—his face draining of all color—Jilly donned her most innocent-looking expression and said, "You have a nice day now, Arthur, all right?"

"Y-yes, ma'am," Arthur stammered, still staring wide-eyed and pale-faced at Jilly.

Jilly held in her giggles until she was well beyond Arthur's range of hearing and then allowed herself just one triumphant snicker. She knew darn well that for the rest of his life Arthur Farley would wonder if it were an accident that Jilly Ramsey had mentioned swimming in the pond only a few days after he and his friends had been caught by some unknown trickster or if Jilly herself had been the very one to pull the prank.

As she approached the general store and tied Romeo's reins to the hitching post nearby, Jilly wondered what Boone would think of her teasing Arthur Farley. Would he join in finding amusement in the boy's discomfort or scold her for nearly giving away their prank? But Jilly smiled, certain that Boone would find humor in the incident.

"Well, well, well . . . if it ain't Mrs. Boone Ramsey herself."

Jilly's amused delight was instantly squelched at the sound of Jack Taylor's voice behind her.

Turning on her heels, however, she forced a

friendly smile and greeted, "Why, yes, it is, Jack Taylor. And good mornin' to you."

Jilly recognized the expression on Jack's face—gloating—and the fact that she knew him well enough to determine what he was feeling made her stomach churn with self-disgust.

"And how's that new husband of yours, Mrs. Ramsey?" Jack asked, his voice so heavy with sarcasm Jilly wanted to slap him again.

"He's just wonderful, Jack, thank you," Jilly answered. She found it strange at first—that a mere two weeks before she would've thought the sun and moon rose and set by Jack Taylor, and now all she saw was a pompous, brainless tomcat standing before her. There wasn't one tinge of feeling in her heart toward him—other than regret.

"Well, if he's so wonderful . . . then why are you here in town all alone?" Jack baited.

Jilly shrugged as if there were nothing strange about a woman coming to town without her husband's escort—because in truth, there wasn't—not in Mourning Dove Creek anyway.

"Oh, Boone's out helpin' the Graham family with somethin'," she answered. "Seems their little girl—"

"Come on, Jilly," Jack interrupted, taking hold of her arm. "Let's have us a little talk, hmmm? Over here where no one can see . . . because I've got some things to say to you."

"Well, I don't have anything to say to you, Jack Taylor," Jilly said, wrenching her arm from his grasp.

"Oh, come on, Jilly," Jack chuckled, however. "Wasn't more than ten days ago you were beggin' me to marry you—sweeter on me than a baby to candy—and now you're gonna stand here and make out like you ain't still?"

"I'm not," Jilly answered. She shook her head, and through narrowed eyes that displayed pure contempt, she continued, "I don't know what I was thinkin' by spendin' my time on you, Jack. There's nothin' at all to you . . . nothin' but thinkin' to yourself that you're somethin' special. But you're not. You're a coward, a snake. I'm just glad Boone rescued me from you before—"

But her words were cut off when Jack suddenly took hold of both her arms and growled, "Don't you talk to me that way! I ain't no coward. I'm just not stupid." He glared at her. "What makes you think I would ever take to just one girl when I can have as many girls as I set my mind to havin'? And anyway, your grandpa forced you to marry Boone Ramsey. I know it. It wasn't your choice."

"Yes, it was," Jilly said. It was the truth, after all. Maybe she'd married Boone out of spite—or, more truthfully, convinced herself that was the reason, at least at first—but she had chosen to marry him.

"I married him because he's the best man I've

ever known," she said as Jack's grip on her arms tightened. "You'll never be half the man Boone is, Jack. You don't have it in you."

"What the hell are you doin'?" Boone roared as he stepped out of the general store carrying a sack of flour. Slamming the sack to the boardwalk, Boone strode so quickly to where Jilly stood that Jack Taylor didn't know what hit him. But Jilly did—Boone's powerful fist.

"You take your hands off my wife, boy!" Boone shouted, reaching down and taking hold of the front of Jack's shirt, pulling him to his feet once more. "Don't you ever touch her!" Boone shouted into Jack's face. Jilly gasped as Boone landed another brutal blow to Jack's jaw—only this time Jack didn't stumble to the ground, because Boone still held the front of his shirt in one hand to keep him on his feet.

"Don't you ever speak to her again without my permission, you hear me, boy?" Boone growled. This time when Boone's fist met with Jack's jaw, Boone let go of Jack's shirt and raised one foot, planting his boot square in Jack's midsection and shoving him backward. Jack stumbled back, bloody-nosed and disoriented, tumbling down into the dirt.

Leveling a trembling index finger at Jack—who lay writhing breathless, bleeding, and in pain on the ground—Boone added, "You're just lucky I didn't lose my temper, you jackass."

Instantly Boone turned to Jilly, his brow puckered with concern. “Did he hurt you, Jill?” he asked.

Jilly shook her head. She couldn’t have admitted to any of the onlookers at the moment, but the pink heat she felt on her cheeks wasn’t embarrassment at Boone’s display or anger with Jack but rather pride that her husband, the handsomest man ever born, had just put Jack Taylor right smack where he belonged—on his hiney there in the dirt.

CHAPTER NINE

"Thank you, Boone," Jilly said as she sat across from Boone at the supper table that evening. All day—ever since Boone had knocked the wadding out of Jack Taylor in front of the general store—Jilly had been overwhelmed with feelings of gratitude and humility.

Though she was sure it hadn't been Boone's intention, not only had he rescued her from Jack's tormenting, but he'd also rescued her reputation as well. She was certain that by the end of the day there wouldn't be a person left in Mourning Dove Creek that would believe Boone Ramsey and Jilly hadn't married for love.

"For what?" Boone asked, spreading a piece of bread with butter.

"For knockin' the waddin' out of Jack Taylor for me," she explained. "I've wanted to do that for . . . well, since . . . since . . ."

"Since he wouldn't marry you and left you to me?" he asked, grinning.

"Yes," she admitted.

Boone chuckled. "Well, you're welcome. But I have to admit, the pleasure was all mine. It felt good to give that jackass what he's had comin'."

"I'm just really thankful you were there," Jilly added.

"Well, we hauled the little Graham girl out of the well pretty quick, and then I remembered the flour can is runnin' low, so I stopped into town to pick some up," he explained.

"And is she all right?" Jilly asked. "The little Graham girl, I mean?"

Boone nodded, taking a bite of his bread. "The water wasn't too deep down in that old well . . . just a foot or so. But she was wet and cold and scared when I got down there to her. Poor little thing. She didn't break an arm or a leg or anything though. She was lucky."

"Well, I'm glad she wasn't hurt," Jilly said. Blushing a little, she added, "And I'm glad you weren't either."

"Oh, I never get hurt," Boone commented. But when Jilly arched one eyebrow with skepticism, he added, "Well, not too often anyhow." He put his bread down on his plate then, dusted the crumbs from his hands, and said, "Hey, that reminds me . . ."

Jilly watched as he stood, slipped his suspenders from his shoulders, and stripped off his shirt. She couldn't help but smile as she watched him stride to the cupboard. She just adored him in his shirtless state.

"Will you clip off these stitches Doc Havasham

put in real quick?" he asked, returning to the table and handing her a pair of small scissors. "They're itchin' me somethin' awful, and I think everything is scabbed together good enough."

Jilly's eyes widened as she accepted the scissors. "You want me to cut the stitches?"

"Yeah . . . if you don't mind," he answered. "You just clip 'em in the middle, and then you can pick them out with your fingernails. All right?"

"But won't that hurt?" she asked, horrified at the thought of causing Boone any pain at all.

Boone shrugged. "Naw," he answered. "But their itchin' is drivin' me loco." Taking hold of his chair, he pulled it away from the table, sitting down backward on it as he straddled the back of it with his long legs. Folding his arms and resting them on the back of the chair, he said, "Okay. Just snip them, and they'll pull right out."

Jilly gulped, stood, and strode to where Boone was sitting. The wound from the ax was healing well, though it would obviously scar. Still, she could see that the stitches were no longer necessary and might actually prove a hindrance to Boone's healing now.

"So just snip them down the middle?" she asked in a whisper as she placed her left hand on his back and readied her right hand that held the scissors.

Boone startled a little and chuckled, "That tickles a bit . . . sorry."

• • •

In truth, Jilly's touch didn't tickle at all; rather, it caused a tremor of ecstasy to travel through him—a sensation he hadn't expected. Instantly Boone wondered whether asking Jilly to remove Doc Havasham's stitches had been a wise choice. Just her touch had sent his thoughts racing to the fact that she was his wife. And wasn't it his right to hold her, kiss her, and take her to his bed?

Just the thought of kissing her again caused his mouth to begin to water with desire. He closed his eyes a moment, trying to think of anything but the kiss they'd shared the day Reverend Dryer had pronounced them man and wife—but he couldn't. Sure, Boone had kissed other women—done his share of sparking in the past. But that one kiss he'd stolen from Jilly Adams the day they'd been married, it had surpassed any kiss he'd ever experienced before. Fact was, he'd spent a lot of time thinking on it—and even more time keeping himself from kissing her again. Boone didn't want to kiss Jilly again unless she wanted him to. And even though he knew that day might never come, he was determined never to take anything from her unless she gave it to him—anything.

Still, as Jilly's small, soft hands worked to remove the stitches from the wound at his back, Boone knew that if he didn't escape soon, his resolve might be entirely vanquished. He wondered whether she realized that her touch felt like an alluring caress. He figured she did not—else she wouldn't be touching him that way.

"You almost done?" he asked, needing to have her move away from him—to quit touching him.

"Almost," Jilly mumbled. "Just this . . . last little . . . there!" she exclaimed at last. "Finished. You're stitchless once more, Mr. Ramsey."

Jilly frowned, confused as Boone nearly leapt up from the chair, mumbled, "Thanks," and then snatched his shirt from the table where he'd tossed it and began putting it on again.

"I-I didn't hurt you, did I?" she asked with concern.

"Nope," Boone answered rather curtly. "I just remembered somethin' I forgot to do out in the barn is all." He grinned at her, but she fancied it seemed forced. "Thanks again, Jill. It feels much better."

Jilly smiled and nodded. "Glad I could do somethin' for you," she said.

As Jilly turned, intending to return the scissors to the cupboard, a loud knock on the front door caused her to startle. "Someone's here," she said.

Boone frowned. "I wonder who it could be. I ain't expectin' anybody. Are you?"

Jilly shook her head and followed him as he strode toward the door.

She stepped back, her breath catching in her

throat as she saw the silver star badge pinned to the vest of the tall, dark-haired Ranger standing in the doorway.

"Evenin', Boone," the man greeted.

"Evenin', Paul," Boone said in response. "I'm guessin' you're gettin' up a posse?"

The Ranger nodded. "Yep. An outlaw named Pete Koon killed a sheriff up north. I figure if we ride all night we might catch up to him."

"All right. I'll saddle up and meet you out front," Boone said without hesitation.

"I appreciate it, Boone. Thanks," the man said.

"Anytime, Paul. You know that," Boone said, accepting the man's offered hand and shaking it.

Boone closed the door and turned to Jilly. "I might be gone a day or two on this," he told her. "Why don't you saddle up and ride into town to your folks' place so you won't be alone out here?"

"But I want to stay home," Jilly explained. And it was true. Boone and his house were her home now, not her grandpa and grandma's place, and she did want to stay home—in the house she shared with Boone.

Boone looked at her like she had crawfish crawling out of her ears. "Home?" he asked. "You mean here?"

"Yes," Jilly answered. "I don't want to leave. I'll be fine here by myself. Goodness knows I have plenty to keep me busy."

"Are you sure?" he asked, however—obviously unconvinced.

Jilly smiled. "Absolutely," she answered. "Now . . . what do you need to take with you? Can I gather some things for you?"

But Boone just shook his head. "Nope. I'll just grab some jerky and biscuits . . . water. Everything else is in my saddlebags."

"Okay, then. I guess all I can do is tell you to be careful, right?" Jilly asked as anxiety did begin to rise in her then.

"I guess," Boone agreed, smiling at her. "But promise me that if you get lonesome or somethin', you'll ride into town and stay with your folks. I'll tell the hands to keep an eye out for you on my way too, all right?"

"All right," Jilly agreed. Then, all at once, she wanted to kiss him—reach out, throw her arms around his neck, and kiss him good-bye! But she didn't. No, she figured that if Boone Ramsey ever wanted to kiss her again, he'd do it—and he hadn't. So she just clasped her hands at her waist and said, "Well . . . be careful, Boone. Chasin' after outlaws is probably more dangerous than haulin' little girls out of wells, right?"

Boone smiled. "Only if you catch up with them."

Boone's parting words had done nothing to reassure Jilly of his safety. Consequently, Jilly found that, even for the warmth of the summer night, she could not fall asleep. All she could manage was tossing and turning as she worried over her husband's well-being. She even caught herself praying the outlaw the Ranger was chasing would elude the posse—that he'd just disappear into the night and the Ranger would give up and send every man home.

But even as she tossed and turned with agitation and worry, her inability to fall asleep allotted her time to think over the events of the past two weeks—to ponder her feelings of those events—to ponder her feelings. Over and over, she thought of her wedding day—of the strange and forced circumstances surrounding it. Yet over and over, Jilly found that she thought of her wedding day with only fond memories—memories that evoked a sensation of joy, relief, and excitement. It seemed the anxiety and fear—the anger and frustration she'd felt that day—had somehow been obliterated from her mind, leaving only feelings of great happiness.

Naturally, this unexpected realization led Jilly to dissecting why she felt only joy whenever she thought of Boone and being married to him. For a long time she lay in her bed thinking and even talking out loud to herself.

"There's only one answer to all of it," she whispered to the evening summer breeze wafting in through her window. "I'm in love with him.

I've actually fallen in love with Boone Ramsey. And I fell in love with him that very day, I think."

It was an emotional revelation to herself, and Jilly felt her eyes fill with tears—felt her tears spill out over her temples and cheeks as she lay in her bed.

"You've always liked him. Admit it to yourself, Jilly," she spoke. "Even when you were a little girl, you favored him . . . always watched him." She paused, rolling her eyes with self-exasperation. "Marched out to his house on Christmas day to give him a silly orange." She wiped tears from her cheeks. "You only tried to convince yourself you didn't like him because you knew there was no hope of ever winnin' him. And then, one day, out of the blue . . . he walks into your grandma's parlor and asks your grandpa if he can marry you." She frowned. "It makes no sense at all, in truth. Why would he do such a thing? Obviously it wasn't for finding you attractive in any way. He hasn't touched you since you married him!"

Jilly exhaled a heavy sigh. She was so tired—so tired of thinking. And yet her mind wouldn't settle down enough to allow sleep to catch her. For a moment, she considered going out to the barn and saddling Romeo. Maybe she should ride to her grandma and grandpa's house—stay there until Boone returned. Maybe in the familiar surroundings of her old room, she'd find she would be able to sleep.

"No. I don't want to leave home," she mumbled to herself, however. And then an idea began to form in her mind. She couldn't sleep for the sake of worrying about Boone—for missing him. And she wondered, if she changed rooms—if she went to lie in Boone's bed instead of hers, where she could perhaps feel closer to him even though he wasn't there—would sleep come to her?

Before she could reconsider her rash actions, Jilly hopped up out of her own bed and padded across the hall to Boone's room. Opening his bedroom window, she smiled as the fragrance of the fields and pastures floated in—as the sound of the crickets' song began to soothe her.

Pulling down the quilt and top sheet on Boone's bed, Jilly snuggled down into their cozy comfort. Nestling her head on Boone's pillow and savoring the scent of fresh green grass, leather, bacon, and lye soap, Jilly sighed. Though she suspected—rather she knew—that sleeping where Boone usually slept wasn't nearly as wonderful as sleeping in his arms would be, she did feel soothed. There was still the matter of the fact she loved him—that it seemed ridiculous that she could after so short a time as they had been married—but as her mind and body began to relax, Jilly figured it was a puzzle that could wait until morning to be solved.

Boone's down-filled pillow was soft—infused with the lingering essence of him—and Jilly soon found herself bathed in a comfortable reprieve from the worries and wondering. As the summer crickets made their music and the fragrant breeze caressed everything it touched, Jilly did drift off to sleep—imagining that she slept not just in Boone's warm, comfortable bed but in the strength and safety of his arms.

CHAPTER TEN

One day without Boone was bad enough. But when one day stretched to two, and then two days stretched to three, Jilly's worry and anxiety over Boone's safety had her as nervous as a cat in a room full of rocking chairs! She found that nothing distracted her from her fears for Boone's sake. And she likewise found that she missed his company so very much that it made her heart ache for him.

Jilly's emotions leapt between anger that Boone had left her to go running off in search of some outlaw and despair in wondering if he were well. One moment she was determined that when he returned, she would demand he never leave her alone to go off with some posse ever again. Then the next she would find herself kneeling beside his bed, praying that he would simply be watched over and returned safely to her.

And yet when at last—after three long days and nights—she heard the gallop of a horse approaching and looked out the kitchen window to see Boone ride up, silhouetted against the sun-set, Jilly found that all her anger at having been abandoned vanished, leaving nothing but pure relief and resplendent joy in its wake.

Still, even as she watched him slowly saunter out of the barn, stop in front of the rain barrel, strip off his shirt, and begin washing the dust and dirt from his face, hair, and torso, her excitement grew. Boone was home, at last! He had come back and would be with her that night! Jilly was glad that, in hoping for Boone's return, she'd prepared a nice supper of fried chicken, potatoes, and freshly baked bread. No doubt her husband would be tired from his travels—whether or not the outlaw had been captured.

Boone smiled at Jilly as he stepped into the house through the back porch door. "Mmmm. It smells good in here," he said.

"I'm glad," she said. Jilly found her heart was all aflutter at seeing him again—that her stomach seemed to be turning somersaults with excitement. "Supper's all ready . . . if you're hungry enough."

"Hungry enough?" Boone chuckled. "I've been eatin' jerky and hardtack for three days! I'm so hungry I could eat *you* up right now!"

Jilly giggled nervously. The three days apart from him, coupled with all the deep soul-searching she'd done, had her feeling like a giddy schoolgirl.

"Well, sit down, and I'll feed you a nice

supper," Jilly said. "Then you can go right to bed if you want. You must be tired." As she prepared a plate for Boone, she added, "Did you catch him? The outlaw?"

"Yep," Boone answered with a tired sigh. "The Ranger and a few other posse members are takin' him out to Yuma prison. But I decided to come on back. I didn't want you out here all alone any longer."

Jilly smiled. "Well, I'm glad you didn't go to Yuma with them," she admitted, setting the plate heaping with chicken and potatoes on the table in front of Boone.

Boone sighed again, and Jilly noted the way his shoulders slumped forward. "I hope I ain't too tired to eat," he mumbled. "All of a sudden I'm plum worn out."

"You probably didn't sleep well, I'm guessin'," Jilly offered, taking her seat across from him. She was so delighted to have him home! All she could seem to do was stare at him.

"Didn't sleep at all till we had him tied up last night," Boone explained. "And even then I only caught a couple of hours. I swear, I can hardly see straight."

Jilly frowned. "Well, I don't like that you're that tired," she said.

Boone looked up with very sleepy green eyes and grinned. "Oh, I'll have a good long sleep tonight and be right as rain in the mornin'."

"Are you sure?" Jilly asked, suddenly feeling fearful. She found that she was worried all over again. Fatigue was a terrible thing. What if Boone still weren't out of danger? What if the posse ride and lack of sleep caused him to come down with some illness or something?

Boone chuckled. "I'm sure," he answered. "And it's kind of you to be concerned."

"Of course I'm concerned! You're my husband!" Jilly exclaimed, far too emotionally.

Boone's eyes widened with astonishment, but he didn't say anything.

Jilly felt silly for allowing herself to tip her hand too much, letting Boone know how much she cared for his well-being. So in an attempt to distract him from any suspicions he might have that she'd realized she'd fallen in love with him, she said, "Why don't you finish your supper, and I'll see that your bed is ready and comfortable for you, all right? Then you can turn right in and get to sleep."

"Okay," Boone answered.

Jilly could feel his suspicious gaze following her as she hurried down the hall. The fact was she couldn't remember how she'd left his bed after sleeping in it for the past nights. And when she entered his room—sure enough—she'd left his bed unmade.

Quickly she straightened Boone's bed, fluffing his pillows and making sure the window was open so the cool evening breeze would freshen the room.

"I find that I'm just too tired to finish my supper, Jill," Boone said from the doorway, startling Jilly.

Whirling around, she said, "Oh, that's fine. You can eat when you're rested up."

"Thank you," Boone said, striding toward her. Jilly held her breath as he stopped right in front of her. Gazing down at her through fatigued but brilliantly alluring eyes, he said, "I missed you, Jill."

Jilly's heart leapt in her chest with delight. And yet she managed to remain outwardly calm and simply said, "I missed you too, Boone."

Boone sighed and grinned a little. "Well, sorry to leave you up alone another night, but I really am wrung out."

Jilly nodded and stepped aside. Boone strode to his bed, sat down, and began struggling to pull off one boot.

"Well, sleep tight . . . and let me know if you need anything, okay?" she said.

"Okay," Boone yawned.

Then as his boots hit the floor and he stood to begin unbuckling his belt, Jilly blushed, said, "Good night then," and took her leave.

An hour passed before the sun had completely set. Another passed before Jilly decided she might as well go to bed. How dull the evenings without Boone had seemed. And the current evening was nothing less than frustrating, for she was desperate for his company—for the conversation and laughter they usually shared.

Nevertheless, with night coming on, Jilly changed from her day dress into her nightgown, brushed her hair, and prepared for bed. Yet as she lay in her bed, she began to worry once more over Boone. He'd appeared so very tired—it disturbed her. Jilly began to wonder if he really were all right. Was he comfortable? Warm enough? Was he breathing, or had the taxing task of riding with the posse robbed him of it?

A strange sense of insecurity began to consume Jilly, and she knew that until she was certain Boone was resting comfortably and well—that he was indeed still breathing—she would never rest herself.

Very quietly, she crept from her bed, across the hallway, and into Boone's room. The moon was full in the night sky, sending bright silver moonbeams through the window to illuminate the room. Jilly was glad, for she could see Boone quite clearly.

Carefully, so as not to wake him, she leaned over him and listened. Yes! She could hear the slow, rhythmic breathing of a man deep in slumber. Relief flooded her, for Boone was well. He looked comfortable enough as well. Though he was not covered by a blanket or even a sheet, he slept on his back, one hand tucked beneath his pillow and the other outstretched at his side. He was wearing only his underdrawers, covering him from the waist to his ankles, and Jilly felt a smile spread across her face as she studied him for a long time.

Boone's hair was tousled, and had it not been for his incredibly large, muscular body, chiseled square chin, and other manly features, he might have been mistaken for a boy who'd been out playing all day. There was an expression of pure peace on his face—an expression Jilly had never seen there before—and it drew her in.

In fact, gazing at his face led her attention to lingering on his lips—to thinking, again, on the kiss he'd given her on their wedding day. Jilly frowned, wondering why Boone had seemed to not mind kissing her the day they were married but never again tried to kiss her since. She thought of the long moments she'd spent sparking with Jack Taylor—the regret and self-disgust that the memory always brought to her. And suddenly she was tired of waiting for the moment that Boone might decide to kiss her again. She wanted to feel his lips pressed to her own—to assure herself that his kiss on their wedding day truly had been as supreme as she remembered.

Knowing he was tired—worn out and unconscious from several nights' lack of sleep—Jilly figured that there was no way a simple kiss would rouse him to wakefulness. He'd been too tired to even eat a good supper, too tired to talk with her, see straight, maybe even too tired to stand. Certainly one tender, soft kiss wouldn't disturb him.

And it didn't. As Jilly leaned over, gently touching her lips to Boone's, he did not even stir in the slightest. This, however, bolstered Jilly's confidence, and instantly knowing that one light kiss would never satisfy her desire to kiss him, she bent and carefully pressed her lips to Boone's once more.

Every inch of her body was alive with bliss at the feel of his lips to hers! She found that kissing him, even when he was unaware she was doing so, was purely exhilarating—caused her heart to beat with a wild rhythm in her chest.

A third time she kissed him, unable to deny herself the pleasure—unable to give him up. Yet this time, even for the deep slumber that owned him, she felt his lips respond to hers—felt him gently kiss her in return. And if she thought the bliss of kissing was overwhelming before, his unconscious response sent her senses whirling.

Boone's eyes didn't open, and he made no sudden moves. Yet Jilly held her breath when she felt his hands suddenly cradling her face when she kissed him a fourth time. This time, she was certain there must be some consciousness about him, for not only was he holding her face between his warm, powerful, yet careful hands—he was kissing her! Really kissing her! And in much the same way he had at their wedding.

"What are you doin', Jill?" he mumbled after a time.

"I-I . . . I-I'm just so glad you're home . . . and I wanted to . . . I wanted to . . ." Jilly stammered.

Boone's eyes opened then—though narrowly—and he stared at her a moment before grinning and saying, "You wanted to see if I'm still a better kisser than Jack Taylor," he finished for her.

"I just . . . I just . . ." Jilly stammered, blushing with humiliation.

"Well, why did you wait until I'm half dead, darlin'?" Boone asked. "I ain't myself right now . . . and that don't seem fair."

"No, no. I only wanted . . ." Jilly continued to stammer.

She gasped, however, when suddenly Boone's hands released her face, his arms banding around her as he pulled her onto him, rolling her over on the bed until he hovered over her.

"You gotta give me a fair chance, Jill," he said, smiling down at her through still very fatigued-looking eyes. "I can put ol' Jack Taylor to shame in every way . . . but not when I'm half dead from ridin' down an outlaw." He chuckled. "But

I'll tell you what . . . I'll give it a try anyhow, all right?"

"Boone, I'm sorry. I didn't mean to . . ." Jilly began.

But a kiss like Jilly had never known or even ever imagined silenced her. As Boone's mouth descended to capture hers in a warm, moist, intimate kiss, Jilly lay breathless beneath him, swept away to unfamiliar and unexpected, yet extraordinary, pleasure!

Again and again he kissed her, coaxing her into accepting and then returning his impassioned affections. Every part of Jilly's insides were trembling uncontrollably! She felt overly warm, but wonderfully so! Over and over her mouth met with Boone's, mingled in a shared exchange of intimate desire, longing, and emotion. Gone was Jilly's self-loathing over allowing Jack Taylor to kiss her—for in comparison to Boone Ramsey's skillful, manly kisses, Jack Taylor's were like being licked by a puppy.

All too soon, however, Boone broke the seal of their lips, and Jilly lay quietly beneath him, struggling to catch a regulated breath.

"You taste better than I even imagined, Jill Ramsey," Boone told her. "And one of these days, when I'm not so worn out, I'm gonna have my fill of you, girl. You hear me?"

"Why haven't you ever kissed me again?" she couldn't help asking, even as he placed a lingering kiss on her neck, causing goose bumps to cover every inch of her body. "Other than on our weddin' day? Why haven't you ever tried to—"

"Because I wasn't sure you'd let me," he interrupted. "And even if you did . . . I wasn't sure I could stop once I'd started."

Jilly smiled, inhaling the sweet scent of his skin at his shoulder.

"Now you go on to bed and quit millin' around," Boone said, rolling to his back once more. "I gotta get me some sleep or I won't be worth a hill of beans tomorrow."

"All right," Jilly agreed, disappointed. She could've lingered in Boone's bed exchanging kisses with him forever!

Quickly she climbed over him and out of his bed. But he caught her wrist and stalled her when she started to walk away.

"And, Jill?" he began.

"Yes?"

"Don't be comin' in like that and kissin' on me unless you intend to stay next time, all right?" he said. "It's too hard on a man. You're damn lucky I'm so worn out and sore from that posse ride."

Frowning in lacking a full understanding of what Boone was going on about, Jilly shrugged and said, "Okay. Good night, Boone. Sleep well."

Boone chuckled, sighed, and said, "I'll try."

Jilly halfheartedly returned to her own room.

Her senses were still quivering from the effects of Boone's kisses. All she wanted was to stay in his bed with him—be held in his arms and kissed all through the night. She couldn't imagine a more wonderful way to drift off to sleep!

And then the ugly imp of doubt began to seep into her thoughts. Boone had kissed her, held her, caressed her—but he'd also been nearly drunk with fatigue. Jilly began to wonder if he would've done the same had he not been so tired. Perhaps what he'd said had been true—that he'd been uncertain as to whether she would allow him to kiss her again. Then again, she couldn't imagine why any woman would refuse a kiss from Boone Ramsey!

Even still, doubt had managed to creep into her thoughts, and there it nested—for hours and hours—until the rooster crowed and the first rays of sunshine glinted on Jilly's bedroom window, causing her eyes to close in search of shade, finally sending her off to sleep.

CHAPTER ELEVEN

The sound of voices woke Jilly from her deep sleep. Sitting up in her bed and rubbing her eyes, the memory of the night before—of Boone's impassioned kisses—washed over her, sending every part of her being soaring with delight and hope.

But her zenith was short-lived, for once more she heard voices coming from outside the house—voices raised in excitement, mingled with the sound of horse hooves.

"Jill!"

Jilly gasped as she looked to her open window to see Boone astride his horse.

"What's goin' on?" she asked, still drowsy with the lingering effects of a deep sleep.

Boone shook his head. "Somebody fell down in the old mine shafts just outside of town, and I'm ridin' out there to help. You go on about your day, and I'll be home soon, all right?"

Jilly was instantly angry. "No! It's not all right! Why do you have to go, Boone? You just got back from that posse ride . . . and before that it was the well and the little

Graham girl! You're gonna get hurt one day!"

But Boone smiled and shook his head. "No, I won't," he assured her. "But I'm flattered that you're worried about me."

"Boone, don't go," Jilly said. "Please . . . I worry so much when you're off doin' somethin' like this."

"I'll be careful, Jill," Boone said, however. "You don't worry and just have yourself a nice breakfast. I'll be back before you know it."

But as he turned and rode away—as three other men on horses joined him—a great and oppressive sense of doom settled over Jilly just like an ominous thunderhead. He'd become too confident! Boone was always the one saving everybody from everything, and it had buoyed up his confidence too much. The mines were treacherous; everybody knew it, and everybody stayed away. Furthermore, Jilly knew that the last time someone had fallen in the mine, he and the man who went in after him ended up dead and buried under fifteen feet of rubble.

Quickly she hopped out of bed and washed her face and hands with the pitcher and bowl on the small table in her room. Brushing her hair, she braided it back as fast as she could and then dressed.

Jilly was glad Romeo was so cooperative when it came to being saddled. It meant that she wouldn't be too far behind the men that had ridden off toward the mines.

"Yah!" Jilly shouted, causing Romeo to bolt out of the barn at a dead gallop.

The tears brimming in Jilly's eyes made it difficult to see, but she still rode hard toward the mines. She had to stop Boone from going after whomever had fallen in. Something was spurring her on—screaming to her mind that she had to stop him. Was it a premonition? Would this be the time that Boone's kind heart and heroics killed him?

Jilly's tears spilled over as fear overtook her. She had to stop Boone! It was all she could think of. He couldn't continue to risk his life for everyone in Mourning Dove Creek. Sure, someone needed to help others—but did it always have to be Boone Ramsey?

She knew what people thought—that he was heroic. But more than that, she suspected they thought Boone was expendable. After all, everyone else in town had families—wives and husbands, children, grandparents. But Boone had had no one for so very long that folks had begun to think it was all right for him to risk his life to save someone else. After all, if something tragic happened to him, who was there to mourn him?

Jilly's fear increased, as did her anger, as she rode. Perhaps not everyone thought Boone was expendable—perhaps no one did. But the way everyone allowed him to risk life and limb over and over again made her suspect that some did. But he wasn't! Boone was more important than anyone—at least to Jilly he was. And now he did have a family to mourn him if tragedy struck—her!

As she rode on, the sound of saddle leather shifting in rhythm with Romeo's gait, the sound of Romeo's breathing ringing in Jilly's ears, she thought of nothing but Boone—of how much and how long she'd loved him. Not for the scant space of two weeks since he'd asked to marry her, but for as long as she could remember, even before she'd taken him that silly orange over ten years before—and she wouldn't lose him! She wouldn't lose him, ever, and certainly not because some fool fell into a mine he shouldn't have been poking around anyway!

"Be careful down there, Clarence," Boone hollered into the mineshaft as he helped lower Clarence Farley. "Them walls will crumble and come fallin' down on you quicker than you think."

"Give him some slack there, Boone," Doolin Adams instructed as he leaned over the hole that had opened up and swallowed Clarence Farley's little brother, Arthur. Turning to glare at Davey Graham and Willy Lillingston, Doolin scolded, "What in the hell were you boys doin' out here anyway? You know how dangerous these old mine shafts are!"

"We didn't know them shafts stretched out this far from the mine's openin'," Willy explained.

"If my mama finds out about this, I'll be skinned alive for sure!" Davey Graham whined.

"Well, you oughta be," Boone grumbled. "You three boys are more trouble than a nest of yellow jackets, I swear."

"I got him!" Clarence hollered from the mine sinkhole. "Haul us on up, Boone! And do it quick. I think Arthur's got a broken arm."

Doolin Adams shook his head. "You best run into town and get your daddy, Mona," he told the Havasham girl who had run into town looking for help in the first of it.

"Yes, sir, Mr. Adams," Mona said as she turned and started running back toward town.

Boone puffed as he worked to help Sam Rutherford haul Clarence and his brother out of the hole. Wrapping the rope around his waist, Boone reached down and took hold of Arthur's good arm when the boy finally broke daylight.

After he'd assisted Clarence out as well, he accepted the handshake his friend offered.

"Thank you, Boone," Clarence said. "It seems you're always around to help everybody out of a pickle."

"Yes, it does seem that way, doesn't it?"

Boone was startled at the sound of Jilly's

voice—even more startled when he turned to see her dismount Romeo and begin storming toward him.

"You have to stop this, Boone Ramsey!" she cried, tears streaming down her face. Boone's eyes widened with astonishment as she placed her small hands on his chest and shoved him backward. "I will die of worry if you don't stop runnin' off to pull every idiot out of every mess they tumble into! Do you hear me?"

"Jill," Boone began, still rattled by his wife's emotional outburst, "the Farley boy . . . he fell into a shaft and—"

"And I'm sorry that he did!" Jilly cried. "But you can't always be the one to risk your life for someone, Boone! I can't take it all the time! I mean, I know it's part of who you are—and I do love that about you—but I'll end up in the asylum if you keep goin' off every day to face danger for the sake of someone else! I swear I'll go crazy!"

Boone glanced to Doolin—to Jilly's grandpa—hoping for some assistance in calming his overwrought granddaughter. But Doolin Adams was too busy chuckling with obvious amusement and simply shrugged.

"And you!" Jilly said, pointing to her grandpa.

"Me?" Doolin asked, surprised and pointing an index finger to himself.

"Yes, you," Jilly confirmed. "You quit eggin' him on, do you hear me?"

"Yes, ma'am," Doolin said—though he was still smiling.

"Jill . . . I'm sorry I worried you so," Boone said, reaching out and taking hold of her arm. "I didn't realize . . . but I guess I do run off a lot and leave you home to worry, don't I?"

"Yes, you do," Jilly said, melting into sobs.

As everyone stood staring at him, Boone simply reached out and gathered Jilly into his arms. "I'm sorry, Jill. I'm sorry. I'll be more thoughtful of your worryin' from now on, all right?"

"All right," she sniffled against him, quite pitifully, and causing all the men standing around to smile with understanding in Boone's predicament.

Boone was more than just astonished; he was awestruck. What had happened? Why was Jilly so upset? Sure, he'd run off a lot of late to help folks, but he'd thought she wouldn't really care too much. Yet then he thought of the night before—the way she'd crept into his room and kissed him. He thought of how she hadn't resisted—not a moment—when he'd taken her in his arms and kissed her the way he'd wanted to kiss her all along. Surely she didn't truly care for him—not as deeply as it appeared she did in that moment. Maybe it was just her way of paying him back for beating the pride out of Jack Taylor. He'd knocked old Jack around a bit, so that now the whole town thought Boone and Jilly were really in love. Maybe this was her way of returning the kindness—making believe that she was so overly worried about him so that the whole town would think she'd married him because she'd wanted to and not because her grandpa had forced her. That must be it—Boone was sure of it.

"Come on, Jill," he said, taking hold of Romeo's reins as the horse approached. "Let's get home, all right?"

He felt her nod against him where her head was pressed to his chest, but she didn't move.

"Come on," he coaxed again. "We're finished here, aren't we, boys?" Boone glanced around to see Clarence Farley's mouth hanging open, Doolin Adams still smiling, and everyone else looking just downright uncomfortable.

"I'm . . . um . . . I'm sure we can finish up here just fine, Boone," Sam Rutherford assured him.

Jilly pulled away from Boone then, angrily brushing her tears from her face. "I'm sorry, you all. I don't know what came over me. I'm just awful tired this mornin'. Boone's been gone for three days, and I didn't get a wink of sleep last night."

When Sam Rutherford and Doolin Adams chuckled, Boone just smiled and took Jilly's arm, leading her to Romeo and helping her to mount.

"I'm right behind you, all right, Jill?" he asked.

She nodded, looked to her grandpa, saying, "Bye, Grandpa," and rode off at a very slow gait.

"So she didn't get a wink of sleep last night, is that it?" Doolin teased Boone.

"That's enough out of you, Grandpa," Boone scolded playfully.

"Well, you best get home and settle her down, Boone," Doolin said, smiling. "When a man's wife is out of sorts . . . the whole world is out of sorts."

"I'm gatherin' that pretty quick," Boone said.

Hurrying to his own horse, Boone mounted and rode out after Jilly. He was still stunned of course—stunned not only by her emotional outburst and apparent concern for his well-being but also in wondering if it were all just a show for the men in town or if it were sincere.

She couldn't face him. She'd been so foolish! Jilly couldn't believe she'd acted so rashly—so emotionally—and in front of her grandpa and several men from town. They must think her the biggest idiot ever born!

And she cringed when she began to imagine what Boone must think of her. He probably thought she'd already lost her senses and needed to be locked up in an asylum! It was why every time she heard the trot of his horse behind her, she spurred Romeo to a faster gait. She just couldn't face Boone!

Jilly knew he could easily ride up and overtake her; his horse was much faster than Romeo. But he didn't, and she was silently appreciative of his sensibilities. As she rode toward home with Boone at her back, Jilly tried to regain control of her chaotic emotions. Whatever was wrong with her? She couldn't fathom it. All she knew was that she was embarrassed at acting so irrationally—and that she loved Boone Ramsey and didn't want him to cast her aside for acting such a fool.

"I'll put him away, Jill," Boone said as they stopped before the barn. "You go on in and . . . and do whatever you need to do, all right?"

Jilly managed to nod and then fled as quickly as she could to the house.

Studying herself in the looking glass in her room, she was further mortified with humiliation. Her cheeks and nose and lips were still red from crying, and her hair was loose and flying every which way. It was a wonder all the men at the site of the mine shaft sinkhole hadn't run away screaming in terror at her horrid appearance—especially Boone.

Trying to calm her nerves, Jilly splashed her face with cool water, brushed her hair, and braided it into a loose braid once more. She heard Boone enter the kitchen through the back porch door—heard him pull a chair out from the kitchen table. He was sitting in the kitchen, waiting for her—and she knew she'd have to face him sooner or later.

Therefore, opting for sooner, Jilly inhaled a deep breath in an effort to gather her courage and left her room to go to the kitchen.

Going to the sink, she worked the pump a moment as she retrieved two drinking glasses from the cupboard. Filling each glass with cool water from the pump, she then carried them to the kitchen table, setting one glass on the table in front of Boone and the other on the table in front of her as she took her seat across from him.

Jilly didn't look at Boone, of course—not at first—not until he said, "So what was that all about?"

Then, feigning ignorance—for in truth, she really did wish the whole thing could just be forgotten—she said, "What was what all about?"

Boone grinned and puffed a laugh. "Were you just givin' back to me for beatin' the snot out of Jack Taylor? Is that it?"

And there it was! Boone had offered her an escape! All she had to do was tell him that, yes, she was returning the favor he'd done for her by beating Jack Taylor down. She didn't have to tell him that his constant heroism for the sake of others frightened her to death—that she worried constantly over his safety. She didn't need to confess that she'd finally admitted to herself that she was in love with him.

Yet Jilly knew that, if she ever hoped to win

any part of Boone Ramsey's true affections, then the time had come for the truth.

And so she answered, "No. I wasn't just returnin' a favor."

"You weren't?" Boone asked, the doubt obvious in his voice.

"No . . . I wasn't," Jilly affirmed. "It really does upset me when you go runnin' off to danger. I really do worry."

Boone sighed with obvious pleasure in her response. Reaching across the table, he took her hand in his and said, "I bargained for you, Jill. You know that, don't you?"

"What do you mean?" she asked, truly confused.

"With your grandpa . . . that day I asked him if I could marry you," Boone began to explain. "I told your grandpa that if he convinced you to marry me, you'd always be taken care of . . . that I'd make sure everything I own, everything I've built, all of it would belong to both of us. That way if anything ever happened to me, you'd be provided for. It's why I went to your grandpa in the first place. I heard him talkin' to Doc Havasham the one night, and he was worried about what would become of you if somethin' happened to him and your grandma. And he didn't want you marryin' up with that jackass Jack Taylor. So I told him . . . I made a bargain with him—that if he made you marry me, then

I'd see that you had everything you would ever need for your comfort and safety."

Tears of heartbreak filled Jilly's eyes, for she realized then that she was nothing more to him than another citizen in Mourning Dove Creek in need of saving. That was all. Boone Ramsey had married her to ease her grandpa and grandma's worries—not because he favored her—not even because he wanted a wife—but simply out of pity.

Yet Boone seemed to misunderstand her tears. "Truly, Jill. Even if somethin' happens to me while I'm out helpin' hunt outlaws or diggin' little girls out of wells, you'll always have a nice home, money . . . and everything you need. It's what I promised your grandpa in the bargain."

"So you just married me out of pity?" Jilly said, tears escaping her eyes to trickle over her cheeks. Snatching her hand from under his, she added, "You felt sorry for me? That's all?"

Boone frowned. "Well, no . . . of course not," he answered. "Like I said, it was a bargain I made with your grandpa. He got the knowledge that you'd always be well cared for, and I got—"

"It's why you didn't haul me to your bed and have your way with me on our weddin' night, isn't it?" she squeaked as the pain in her heart began to branch out into her limbs and throat. "You just married me out of pity!"

Boone's frown deepened then, and he growled, "So what if I did, Jill? Why did you marry me? Huh? Not out of choice, and certainly not because you wanted to. You married me out of pure spite aimed at that jackass you'd been sparkin' with for a month down by the creek. So what's worse, huh? Marryin' out of spite? Or out of pity? Answer me that!"

Shoving his chair back from the table, Boone stood, glaring down at her as his broad chest rose and fell with the labored breathing of anger.

"For your information, Boone Ramsey," Jilly cried, standing up from her own chair and glaring at him, "I married you for the same reason I brought that silly orange to you one Christmas ten years ago!"

"Oh, now you're gonna claim you married me out of pity too?" he grumbled.

"No!" Jilly sobbed. "I married you because I love you! I've loved you for as long as I can remember! I just couldn't let myself admit it because . . . because—"

"Don't you stand there and tell me you love me unless you really mean it, Jill," Boone interrupted as moisture filled his beautiful green eyes. "I made myself a promise ten years back . . . that that little girl who brought me that orange on Christmas . . . that I'd always watch out for her, no matter what I had to do. And that Jack Taylor, he was gettin' his hooks deeper and deeper into you, and I knew I had to do somethin'. So I went to your grandpa, and I bargained for you, Jill. That's what I did! I bargained with Doolin Adams for the hand of his granddaughter. He got the peace of mind that you would always be cared for . . . but aren't you at all curious about what I got?"

"I know what you got, Boone," Jilly wept. "You got to be the hero again . . . to pull a little girl out of a well or a little boy out of a rain-swollen creek. That's what you got."

"No," Boone argued, however. "I got *you,* Jill. I love you! I've wanted you since you were old enough to want."

But Jilly's heart was too busy breaking to hope in that moment. "Is that so?" she asked.

"That's so," Boone answered.

"Then why didn't you, if you care for me so much, if you really wanted me . . . then why didn't you want me to share your bed the night we were married?" she asked.

"Because *you* didn't want *me,* Jill," he answered. "You weren't ready for me to love you then. You were still gettin' over Jack Taylor."

"But I wasn't!" Jilly confessed wholeheartedly. "I was over Jack Taylor before I got back home from tellin' him Grandpa had promised me to you! I still don't completely understand what I was thinkin' where Jack was concerned. Maybe . . . maybe it was simply that . . . if I couldn't have the man I wanted, I thought I had to settle for the man I could get."

Boone's eyes narrowed. "You're lyin'," he accused.

"I'm not," Jilly assured him, shaking her head. "You are."

"No, I'm not," Boone growled.

"Then prove it," Jilly challenged.

"You prove it," Boone challenged in return.

"You prove it first," Jilly countered. "You're the one who claims you went to my grandpa because you wanted me and didn't want Jack Taylor to have me. So you prove it first."

Jilly could feel the contention between her and Boone dissipating—felt her heart cease in its misery and begin to hope once more.

"All right, I will," Boone mumbled.

Jilly gasped as Boone stepped up directly in front of her, slipped his suspender straps from his shoulders, and stripped off his shirt, tossing it to the table.

Instantly she was in his arms—held tight against the warmth of his firm, muscular body—his mouth having captured hers in a hot, ravenous kiss. Jilly didn't pause in responding, for there was no reason to pause. Boone Ramsey loved her! She could feel that he did—taste that he did. And when she allowed her hands to gently caress the breadth of his shoulders to travel up the back of his neck to his hair—as she felt a tremor travel through his body and he increased the intimacy of their kiss—she melted to him—surrendered her heart and body to his.

"I love you, Jill," Boone mumbled against her mouth. "I . . . I maybe didn't understand just how much that day I went to your grandpa . . . not at first. But when I left your grandpa standin' there on the front porch—walked right past you and you looked at me when I greeted you and said, 'Afternoon, Mr. Ramsey'—that was the moment I had to admit to myself the real reason I'd asked your grandpa for you . . . because I love you . . . and I want you for me . . . for mine."

"I love you too," Jilly whispered. "And . . . and I think Grandpa already knew it the day you talked to him about me."

"Why do you think that?" Boone asked.

Jilly smiled. "Because he agreed to your bargain, Boone," she answered. "And he never would have if he hadn't already known my secret about you . . . that I've loved you for simply ever. I mean, think about it—an eight-year-old girl givin' away the best part of Christmas mornin'?"

"Jill," Boone began, "I promise . . . come this Christmas, I'll show you what the best part of Christmas mornin' really is."

Jilly giggled, "The orange, of course."

"Nope," Boone said, taking her by the waist, lifting her, and hefting her over one shoulder.

As Boone laid Jilly on her bed on her back,

hovering over her like a wolf that had captured its prey, he smiled and said, “This,” as his mouth claimed hers in a kiss that proved he’d loved her all along.

EPILOGUE

Taking the beautiful, ripe orange from its hiding place in the drawer in the small table next to their bed, Jill Ramsey turned to her husband and said, “Merry Christmas, Boone Ramsey!”

Boone chuckled as he took the orange she offered. “You couldn’t wait until the sun was up and we were out of bed?” he asked, smiling at her as he studied the orange.

“No,” Jill answered. “And do you know why not?”

“Because we promised to be to your grandma and grandpa’s house for Christmas breakfast?”

“No, silly,” Jill laughed. Taking the orange from him, she pressed her thumbnail into the soft orange skin and began to peel it back.

“Then why?” Boone inquired, raking a hand back through his hair. “It’s so early. You’re up before the rooster, darlin’.”

“Because, Boone Ramsey,” Jill began to explain as she placed the orange peelings on the side table and separated a segment of orange from the rest, “I’ve been waitin’ four months to do this.”

Then placing the orange segment between her teeth so that half of it was in her mouth and the other half was protruding from it, she leaned over her husband and said, “Now kiss me.”

Boone smiled. “Oh, I see,” he mumbled as he took his wife’s shoulders, pulling her to him. The moment their mouths met, Jill bit into the orange wedge, sending the sweet, cool juice from the wedge of orange to meld with their kiss.

“It’s an orange kiss,” Jill explained as she pulled away from Boone and separated another wedge of orange for them. “It’s our new Christmas tradition . . . orange kissin’.”

“I like it,” Boone mumbled as he gathered her in his arms, rolling her over so that he lay on top of her as they shared another wedge. “It’s my favorite Christmas tradition.”

Jill giggled. “It’s only the first time we’ve done it,” she reminded him. “How can it be your favorite tradition already?”

“Well then, it’s my favorite Christmas gift,” he said, kissing her again.

“Are you sure of that?” Jill asked him, placing another orange wedge in her mouth.

“Oh, I am,” Boone assured her, kissing her again.

Jill sighed with feigned disappointment. “Well, then I guess I’ll have to save the other gift I have for you until later,” she said.

“I don’t need another gift,” Boone said,

kissing her throat. “Other than you on Christmas mornin’, I mean.”

Jill giggled, set the orange on her pillow, and wrapped her arms around her handsome husband. “Not even if it’s a gift you’re givin’ me too?”

“But that’s what I mean. I get you on Christmas mornin’, and you, my little orange kisses wife, get me.”

Jill laughed. “No, I mean somethin’ else. I have somethin’ else to give to you.”

Boone smiled, brushed the hair from Jill’s face as he smiled down at her, and asked, “What?”

Jill gazed into her husband’s eyes a moment—marveling at the fact that she saw her own reflection in their brilliant green. She loved Boone more and more every day, even though each night as she drifted off to sleep safe and warm in his arms, she thought it would be impossible to love him more. But then, whenever she awoke, she always did.

“Well, it won’t really be arrivin’ for another five months or so . . . and of course Doc Havasham can only give me an estimation of when it will arrive . . .”

Jill watched with delight as understanding washed over Boone.

“A baby?” he asked in an awed whisper. “Are . . . are you gonna have a baby, Jill?”

“Yes, Boone . . . I am,” she answered.

Jill was astonished then as she continued to

look at Boone, for she hadn't expected to see moisture gather in his eyes the way it was.

"Are you happy, Boone?" she asked, worried for a moment that perhaps he wasn't.

"I am, Jill," he said. Rolling off her, he placed his hand over her tummy. "I am." He shook his head in wonderment. "Every night I go to bed thinkin' that I can't possibly love you any more than I already do. But then I wake up and feel you next to me, watch you breathe as you're still sleepin' sometimes . . . and I realize that I do love you more and more every day. And now . . . now I can't even imagine this, Jill . . . a baby . . . our baby. I don't think I've ever been this kind of happy before." He paused, kissed her cheek, and gazed at her with the moisture of pure joy still lingering in his eyes. "Thank you for lovin' me. I don't need any more than that . . . just knowin' that you love me. Everything else is pure luxury, the way I see it."

"Even orange kisses on Christmas mornin'?" she asked.

"Even orange kisses on Christmas mornin'," he repeated, caressing her cheek with the back of his hand. "You're the sweetest treat I know, darlin'. Even sweeter than orange kisses on Christmas mornin'."

Jill smiled, reached out, and caressed the breadth of his strong shoulders. "Is that so?" she teased.

"That *is* so," Boone answered.

"Then prove it," Jill flirted with her husband.

Boone laughed, picked up the orange from Jill's pillow, and tore away another segment. Leaning over her, he said, "Oh, I will," and then put the orange segment between his teeth and kissed her.

AUTHOR'S NOTE

Way back in the olden days (i.e., 1991–1996), when I was writing my books as Christmas and birthday gifts for close friends, most of my books were about as long as this one, *A Bargained-For Bride*. Being a young wife and mother—a lot younger than I am now, anyway—I wrote my books by stealing ten minutes here and twenty to thirty minutes there. And being that I didn't really have a lot of time to write, my books continued to be novella size.

In fact, it wasn't until 1996 that I found my time and attention span were both long enough to finish a full-length novel—*The Heavenly Surrender*. But even as I began writing full-lengthers (*The Visions of Ransom Lake*, *Shackles of Honor*, *Dusty Britches*, etc.) I found that, on occasion, I needed a break from writing the longer stories—from riding the draining emotional roller coasters with my characters in the novel-lengthers. So in between novels, I'd write a novella here and there. *Sudden Storms*, the original novella-length *Weathered Too Young*, and *The Rogue Knight* gave me those quick reprieves from writing the longer novels.

Now, also along the journey of writing, I inadvertently found myself working part-time from home for about a year for another author—a published author—Orson Scott Card (Scott, as family and friends called him). I didn't do much for Scott—just basically policed the youth poetry section on his website. Teens could post their poetry for critique by other teen poets, and I just had to make sure nothing inappropriate was posted and that no one was posting cruel comments. Remember, this was back when we all still had dial-up modems, so it took me a couple of hours a day.

During this time (1996–1997), Scott read a couple of my stories and encouraged me to publish. He even wanted to publish them himself through his own publishing company. But I still had small children and didn't really want to pursue it at the time. Also, Scott had some things arise that began taking up a lot of his time too. So we both went merrily along our separate paths.

However, one thing Scott Card did mention to me before I quit working for him was that he believed e-books were going to be the future. Remember, this was back in, like, 1998—so I couldn't even conceive that people would ever give up tangible books in favor of e-books. So I guess we know how smart I was *not,* right?

Jump ahead a bit to 2004. By this time, I had

had several books published and was pretty overwhelmed with the whole book business. Enter Marnie Marcus—a friend of my sister's whom I had gotten to know online. Marnie called me one day with a suggestion. Having begun to hear little whisperings of the same thing Scott Card had stated to me years before—that e-books would soon be up and coming—Marnie suggested I allow one of my older novella-length books to be available to my readers as an e-book version.

Yes, I *did* laugh. I thought she was crazy! Nuts! Off her rocker! Who would read a book on their computer? Seriously?

Yet as Marnie explained the process to me, I began to think, "Hmm . . . it might give the readers something to read between the book releases of full-length novels—a 'quick fix' of romance reading, so to speak."

And so *Sudden Storms* became an e-book—and it soared! I couldn't believe it! Even as readers were writing to my customer service lady, asking, "What in the world is an e-book?" *Sudden Storms* was being downloaded like hotcakes! (Hmmm . . . that metaphor needs work.) Readers loved the quick, easy, get-it-right-this-minute e-book fix.

Being that they were so instantly popular, more of my older, novella-length works were published as e-books—but as e-books only. In fact, during this time of my writing and publishing career, I would often write novellas just for the purpose of pleasing those readers who wanted e-books as well as print books. *Love Me*, *The Prairie Prince*, the novella-sized *Saphyre Snow*, *Sweet Cherry Ray*, the first and much smaller version of *The Highwayman of Tanglewood*—all these titles were originally released in e-book format only.

But I so enjoyed writing the smaller titles! Though they were just as emotionally involving for me, the ride wasn't as long, you know? They kept my attention span from getting bogged down, and they lightened my workload somewhat.

But then Scott Card's wisdom and prophetic smarts kicked in. Amazon birthed the Kindle, and the whole world changed forever. What Scott had predicted years and years before began to roll forth.

Skipping all the business nonsense, the fact that I had been published by another publisher and self-published long before self-publishing hit the stance it now has, let's just say, it rocks a business's world when something so epic as what Amazon began to institute takes hold and flies. With so many indie authors now (indie being short for "independent," or self-published), e-books are thicker than fleas on a hound dog! In a venue I was an explorer and entrepreneur in, I found that I missed printed books. I personally still prefer a printed book. I don't even own an electronic reading device yet (at least not in September of 2013).

Thus, while everyone was jumping on the e-book bandwagon, I found that I wanted to do what I could to make sure printed books endured as well. It's one reason you can find hardcover editions of most of my novel-lengthers on my website. Therefore, I began sticking to writing novel-lengthers—because novel-lengthers make better hardcover editions.

And so, there I went, skipping along (stressing to the hilt!) and writing only novel-length books. Until, that is, the "*Midnight Masquerade* Incident of 2012–2013." If you've read my book *Midnight Masquerade*—or had to wait months before it arrived in your mailbox so that you *could* read it—then you know what I'm talking about. The gastric juices are flooding my stomach just *thinking* about it, so I won't go there again. The point is, I became very discouraged and began feeling like I could never write another novel ever (for a ton of reasons).

Until one day, "ZING!" went my brain! I remembered how much I used to love writing novella-length stories—how they were kind of a quick-fix for readers, little shots of romance candy, you know? I also wondered why in the world I'd ever quit writing novellas.

Well, truth be told, I'd quit for many reasons—not limited to but including the diminishing demand for print books and the crazy sick pricing messes where e-books are concerned on the big e-book selling sites.

But the more I thought about it, the more I thought, "What the heck? I used to love writing novellas, and readers loved reading them . . . so why did I ever stop? I'm starting again! I'm going to write a novella. Actually, I'm going to write three. And I'm going to call them the Novellas of Summer 2013!"

Well, I wrote my first novella for the Novellas of Summer 2013—but then the *Midnight Masquerade* Fiasco of 2013 hit! (The *Midnight Masquerade* Fiasco of 2013 is part of, but not all of, *The Midnight Masquerade Incident of 2012–2013* . . . just to clear things up! Ha ha!) Ugh! (Again, if you waited an eon to receive your copy of *Midnight Masquerade*, you know what I'm talking about, right?) So due to the glitches in the release of *Midnight Masquerade*, my first Novella of Summer 2013, *A Good-Lookin' Man*, was delayed—as were the releases of the other two, *A Bargained-For Bride* and *The Man of Her Dreams*. (Ironically, the delays are why I was able to add this part of the Author's Note to this book.)

Why did I babble on and on about this whole "why I quit writing novellas and then started writing them again" thing? In truth, I have no idea! I think I just wanted to give you a little bit of insight into why Boone and Jilly's story was told "novella style." Their story is one I've wanted to tell for so long, but it always lingered in my mind novella style, so I kept putting it off. But when I decided to give myself (and you) some quick-fix romance candy and a break from novel-lengthers (you know, after all the *Midnight Masquerade* drama of 2013), I knew it was time for me to finally share Boone and Jilly's romance with you. So I really hope you liked it!

Meanwhile, I'm off to finish my newest novel-lengther. Wish me luck! ☺

~Marcia Lynn McClure

A BARGAINED-FOR BRIDE TRIVIA SNIPPETS

Snippet #1—You know the first scene in the book when little Georgie Lillingston falls into the creek? Well, that scene was actually inspired by a couple of real-life events. The first is my mom's little bucket. The story of my mom's little bucket was always sad to my sister and me. Mom didn't have many toys, being that she lived on an isolated ranch in Colorado during the Great Depression. Rural life was simple, and luxuries, like toys, were few. So when my mom was playing by the "crick" and the current swept away her little bucket when she tried to fill it with water, my Grandpa States chased it way downstream in an attempt to retrieve it. Mom always says she can still see her dad running down the creek bank trying to catch up with that little bucket. But in the end, the bucket was lost. So in thinking about Mom's sad little bucket story, I got to thinking about how thankful I was that she didn't fall into the creek that day with her bucket, right?

That line of thinking led me to thinking about the arroyos we have here in Albuquerque—and about all the tragic losses that have happened in them. You see, we have these flash floods here in New Mexico. It doesn't even have to be raining right where you are, but if it's raining somewhere else, sometimes you'll hear this roar of rushing water, look into the arroyo, and see a river of rapids coming down it. (Oh, just in case you're not familiar with arroyos—they are sometimes natural and sometimes manmade, basically ditches or canals that are routed through the landscape to divert these flood waters.) Back in the '80s, kids had taken to skateboarding in the large, cement arroyos in the city. Several teenagers were swept away by flash flood waters moving anywhere from twenty to forty miles per hour. There was one incident that was caught on camera in the late '80s; a boy had been washed down an arroyo, and some firefighters had raced downstream and flung a line across the arroyo. One firefighter had hooked himself to it and pulled himself to the middle of the raging water. Miraculously, when the boy came washing toward him, the firefighter managed to get an arm around him. But before he could secure him, a huge lounge chair came washing down in the raging water, knocked the boy loose from the firefighter's hold, and swept him away. The boy was not saved; his body was recovered down where the arroyo waters emptied into the Rio Grande River. It was a horrible incident—tragic and very haunting.

Growing up in Albuquerque, storytellers used to actually come to the elementary schools and tell the story of La Llorona—The Weeping Woman. It was said she roamed the ditch banks, canals, and arroyos looking for her drowned children. It was said that La Llorona (pronounced *Lah Yo-rro-nah*) would snatch children away and drown them if she found them wandering on the banks of the ditch, canals, and arroyos. Creepy, horrible way to keep kids away from the ditches in Albuquerque, right? When my kids were in school here and people were being washed away in arroyos to drown, there was an ad campaign featuring the "Ditch Witch" with the slogan, "Ditches are deadly! Stay away!"

Anyway, now you know what inspired the scene when poor Georgie Lillingston falls into the rain-swollen creek and is eventually saved by Boone Ramsey.

Snippet #2—So here's the thing about the Christmas orange Jilly gave to Boone the year his parents died. Like most Americans (I think) Santa Claus always left an orange or tangerine in the toe of my Christmas stocking (my little sister's too, of course). He always left an orange or satsuma (we call them Cuties down here in

New Mexico) in the toe of my kids' Christmas stockings too.

When I was still a child but old enough to really know Santa Claus, his history, and good intentions, I asked my mom why Santa always left us an orange or a tangerine in our stocking. I mean, it was lovely and always fun to find—and my stocking would never have seemed the same without it—but I didn't know the reason for it, other than simple tradition. Come to think of it, at our church Christmas socials, when Santa Claus would come and one of his helpers would hand each child a brown paper sack filled with peanuts and candy as he or she hopped down from Santa's lap, there was always an orange or tangerine in the bag too—just like the ones Santa left in our stockings. I always just assumed that Santa Claus was nothing if not consistent and very traditional.

Of course, my mom did answer my question about the orange in our stockings. She explained that when she was a little girl, Santa had always left an orange or tangerine in the toe of her Christmas stocking as well. It was always just as fun for her to dig down through the unshelled peanuts, walnuts, hazelnuts, almonds, Brazil nuts (my favorite!), and candy to find the orange in the toe of her stocking. Therefore, Santa had always put an orange or tangerine in the toe of my Christmas stocking, just as he had put them in the toes of her and my dad's Christmas stockings when they were kids. I was already smart enough to know that Mom and Dad receiving an orange for Christmas as children growing up during the Great Depression must've been a rare and wonderful treat indeed—and I left it at that.

In fact, one of my favorite episodes of the currently popular sitcom *The Middle* is an episode entitled, "A Simple Christmas." The orange in the toe of a Christmas stocking makes Frankie (the mom) realize that things need to be simplified in their family Christmas. She feels her kids don't appreciate the orange the way she did—the way her grandmother did when an orange was the only thing she received in her stocking at Christmas. Therefore, Frankie and her husband, Mike, sit down with their three children to explain that they're going to have a simple Christmas—"To truly experience the orange." (Ha ha! I love that line!)

Naturally, the children, Axl, Sue, and Brick, are distraught, thinking that their parents don't plan on giving them any gifts.

Brick asks, "What's the orange?"

Axl then answers, with great dramatics and irritation, "You remember . . . from our stockings . . . that stupid orange from when mom used to live on the prairie and all she got was that stupid orange for Christmas."

I love that scene! And even though it's funny,

it really does ring true to me. I always worry that one day "Santa" will stop leaving oranges in stockings and another sweet, traditional part of history will be lost. But again, I digress.

So back to the orange thing. Over the years, I'd seen a children's book floating around entitled *Christmas Oranges*. But believe it or not, I've never read it. I think it just didn't draw me in for some reason. I loved oranges at Christmas, used them as part of the stocking tradition in our home, and that was enough for me. That is, until Jilly gave the orange to Boone that bright, cool, and crisp Christmas day so long ago.

A moment or two after I'd finished writing the scene where Boone mentions the orange and Jilly reminisces over the event, my curiosity suddenly spiked, and I wanted to know more about the orange in Christmas stockings tradition. The first thing I did was look up a synopsis of the children's story *Christmas Oranges*. I'm guessing you already know the story about the little orphan boy, Jack, who is looking so forward to receiving his Christmas orange from St. Nicholas. But Jack makes a mistake and is punished by having his Christmas orange stripped away by some mean old lady in the orphanage. However, on Christmas morning, he is awakened by a soft hand slipping something into his and discovers that the other boys in the orphanage have each broken their own Christmas oranges into segments—gifting

Jack one segment each so that he too had an entire, lovely, delicious Christmas orange. It's a lesson in forgiveness and love, a truly tender and sweet story. But I figured that couldn't be all of it, right? After all, Santa Claus has been leaving oranges in the toes of Christmas stockings for more than a hundred years, the way I figured it. So I searched a bit further.

It turns out that the Christmas orange tradition dates back as far as good old Saint Nicholas himself. I couldn't find a true, sure date on the legend of the oranges, but the story goes like this. Long, long ago, a poor widowed man had three very beautiful daughters. Indeed, though his daughters were lovely, they were as poor as church mice, thus having no dowries. The poor man was ever so worried about what would become of his daughters when he died. It was a very heavy burden on his heart, for he loved his three daughters more than himself.

Well, one day, Saint Nicholas was passing through the village where the poor man and his daughters resided. A group of villagers stood talking about the poor man and his beautiful, albeit destitute, daughters, and Saint Nicholas overheard their conversation. Saint Nicholas wanted to help, but the villagers told him that the poor man would never accept charity. Yet Saint Nicholas was not to be discouraged.

Late that night, as all the villagers slept, Saint

Nicholas crept down the chimney of the home of the poor man and his daughters. There he found that the daughters had hung their stockings from the mantle to dry after having been washed. Drawing three bags of gold from his pocket, Saint Nicholas dropped one bag of gold into one stocking of each set of stockings. Then Saint Nicholas went on his way.

When the poor man and his daughters awoke the next morning, finding the three bags of gold, they were overjoyed. The three girls, each having her own dowry at last, were soon married, and everyone lived happily ever after.

Who knew, right? Well, obviously everybody but me! I guess sometimes the story is told that it was balls made of gold that Saint Nicholas left in the girls' stockings, and that makes even more sense—that a bright, happy orange in the toe of a Christmas stocking represents Saint Nicholas' care and love for others. Again, who knew?

The whole Christmas stocking tradition stems from an old Germanic/Scandinavian story where children left their boots out filled with straw, carrots, and sugar for the Norse god Odin, to feed his flying horse. Once his flying horse had eaten what the children had left in their boots for him, Odin would fill the boots with candy and gifts as his thanks for their kindness toward his horse.

Seriously, once I get started on something, I could go on forever—so I'll stop now. However, just in case you are an ignoramus like me, I thought you might like to know the very beginnings of why Santa always leaves an orange or tangerine in the toe of a child's Christmas stocking. I like oranges in Christmas stockings all the more now. (And if you see old, old drawings and things of Saint Nicholas, he's often depicted with three golden balls or gold coins. Fun, huh?)

Snippet #3—The truth is I did get dumped once. And I deserved it! The story of the time I got dumped was what inspired the thread in *A Bargained-For Bride* where Jilly is so disgusted, disappointed, and angry at herself for the whole "Jack Taylor" thing. I was in college at the time, and a bunch of my friends in one of the dance bands I sang in kept telling me that this one guy really liked me. They kept pressing me to date him, listing all his great qualities, and pointing out how cool and hot he was. And he was cool and hot—super cool, in fact! So when he walked up to me a few days before the Valentine's Day dance and said, "You *will* be my girlfriend, and I'm taking you to the Valentine's Day dance," I thought, *What the heck?* After all, he was cool and hot, right? To make a long story short—and I do want to point out that I did like the boy—he and I became a couple. He was tall, tall, tall and way, way, way cool, and all the girls I knew wanted to be his girlfriend. So we dated awhile, and I felt kind of crummy for sort of leading him on and allowing him to think things were more serious between us than they really were, you know? But then something would happen, like we'd go to the dance club and suddenly a guy would walk up to us and hand us some sort of prize because we were the best dancers or the coolest-looking couple (because of him, I'm *sure*), and I'd think, *Well, he is cool and hot, and I do like him,* and I'd keep being his girlfriend. However, when he had to be gone for about ten days on a tour with another band, he called me every day at first, wrote me cards and letters, and promised he'd call the minute he got home. Now there's a lot more to this story, including the fact that he ended up bunking in at one home during the band's tour with another guy I liked—and, boy, was I sweating it out—because I hadn't told this guy that I was even dating the band guy! (I was an idiot for about a month there!) Anyway, about four days before my cool, hot boyfriend was due to return, he stopped calling me every day. I got suspicious because I knew there was this gorgeous girl on tour with him who was a little older and really, really after him like a cougar to her prey! And I began to grow suspicious. Sure enough, when cool, hot guy arrived home (and I knew he was home because all the other band guys were home), he didn't call. I waited and waited, and still he didn't call.

And did my heart start to break? Nope! Instead I found that I was enraged—enraged not at him but at myself! I called him up, and he came over with his head hanging with the guilt that he'd cheated on me with this gorgeous cougar girl (she was really only twenty-one at the time ☺) and wanted to break up. Well, I flipped my lid! I flipped my lid at him—but really, inside myself, I was flipping my lid at myself. I was angry at myself, not hurt. We broke up, and he felt bad—but I felt worse! (I still remember the song that was playing when we broke up in my dorm room that day—"Almost Over You" by Sheena Easton.) I was a creep! Though I liked him well enough, I'd really only dated him for fun and because some other people thought I was crazy not to. Even my best friend, Sandy, had scolded me for dating him—but sometimes we have to learn life-lessons the hard way, you know? And I learned so, so, so much from that incident. I always felt so bad about it all—in fact, I still do. As well I should! But then I remember that we did have a lot of fun together and that he did dump me in the end, so I kind of hope it all came out in the wash, you know? Oh, but I do want to make the point that my cool, hot boyfriend was *nothing* like Jack Taylor, okay? He was a great guy and still is! I'm ever thankful to him for the life-lessons he helped me learn and for the maturity I gained after going through what we went through together. He's a great guy, and I'm not just saying that. (By the way—he's still ultra cool!)

Snippet #4—Now, as you know, I *love* to find out where certain clichés, metaphors, and sayings come from. Furthermore, when using one in a book, I like to make sure it was actually used during the time period in which the story takes place. So when I used the phrase "naked as a jaybird" in *A Bargained-For Bride*, I got to thinking, "Okay . . . so jaybirds aren't even naked. So what's up with that?"

It seems that in the nineteenth century, "jay" referred to a person who was either gullible, a simpleton, or a hick—thus the term "jaywalk," referencing a "country bumpkin" or "hick" weaving here and there through city streets looking up at tall buildings and such and paying no heed to traffic. Although this explanation dates the phrase as probably used in the nineteenth century and therefore okay to reference in *A Bargained-For Bride*, it didn't really explain the "naked" part—because I highly doubt that rural people walked around gawking at tall buildings in the nude, especially in the nineteenth century. So I moved on.

I then found that all literal jaybirds, like blue jays and such, are born with hardly any down at all and looking quite naked. Thus, "naked as a jaybird." Hmm. But it still wasn't a satisfactory explanation.

So, there's also the fact that new felons are often called "birds"—and that when they enter prison, they are stripped of everything and processed for jail. Again, "naked as a jaybird."

In the end, I discovered that this is one phrase that really doesn't have a fulfilling, definitive answer. And though that frustrates me, I've been able to let it go—though I think the baby bird analogy is probably the best. Don't you?

ABOUT THE AUTHOR

Marcia Lynn McClure's intoxicating succession of novels, novellas, and e-books—including *Shackles of Honor*, *The Windswept Flame*, *A Crimson Frost*, and *The Bewitching of Amoretta Ipswich*—has established her as one of the most favored and engaging authors of true romance. Her unprecedented forte in weaving captivating stories of western, medieval, regency, and contemporary amour void of brusque intimacy has earned her the title "The Queen of Kissing."

Marcia, who was born in Albuquerque, New Mexico, has spent her life intrigued with people, history, love, and romance. A wife, mother, grandmother, family historian, poet, and author, Marcia Lynn McClure spins her tales of splendor for the sake of offering respite through the beauty, mirth, and delight of a worthwhile and wonderful story.

Center Point Large Print
600 Brooks Road / PO Box 1
Thorndike, ME 04986-0001 USA

(207) 568-3717

US & Canada:
1 800 929-9108
www.centerpointlargeprint.com